HEAT

NEW YORK TIMES BESTSELLING AUTHOR
ERIN McCARTHY

CHAPTER 1

love women. I love everything about them, from the way they laugh and flirt to the way they break underneath me when I'm stroking inside their warm heat. I love the way they move, hips swaying and rolling when they walk, whether it's fuck-me heels, flip-flops, or badass motocross boots. I love the way they smell, like peaches and strawberries, suntan oil, and tangy sweet pussy.

Size, shape, ethnicity don't matter to me. What draws my eye is *their* eye. When we lock on to each other in that first initial gaze, what do I see? Are they a good time? A girl who laughs, who has confidence, who knows what she wants? What they almost always want is me. Because I'm a charming bastard with a big cock and an even bigger ability to flirt. I was born to love women.

And I love them every chance I get.

There is only one woman I've ever wanted that I couldn't have. And as I stood backstage in my suit, wearing a wireless mic, and carrying a gun, I watched her standing ten feet away from me in a tiny sequined bodysuit.

Miranda Bartello.

As I stared, drinking in the sight of her after all these years, I asked my co-worker at Miami Security, Ryan Harris, "You ever feel like there was one woman you missed out on? Like the hit you couldn't have quit if you tried, but you never got a chance?"

"Nope."

I glanced over at him. Ryan was an ugly guy, big, broad, probably close to six foot five, with a nose that had seen too many fists. He was a quiet guy, solid, loyal. He was also annoying because I almost believed him. "You're a liar."

He just shrugged. "I always dated the same kind of women, and they weren't exactly hard to get."

"So you only hit on a sure thing?"

"Pretty much."

Decent strategy for a guy who had zero charm. But Ryan had a girlfriend now, a smart girl who appreciated that he was a guy who would have your back no matter what. I liked that she got that about Ryan. The big lug deserved to be happy.

Miranda turned and glanced our way. Even from twenty feet, I could feel the pull of her. She was even more beautiful now than I remembered. She had polish to her and a maturity to her face. Her cheekbones were more pronounced, her eyes appeared larger in her face. Whether it was age or makeup, I didn't know, but to me, she had always been a freaking goddess. Now wearing a gold sparkly bodysuit and heels that made her sexy legs go on for miles, her blond hair tumbling down her back, I felt a tightness in my gut and a swelling in my cock.

It was a shock to see her.

Three years was a long time.

But I had known that I might see her here. Hell, I'd been hoping I would. Craving a glimpse of her. Now I was feeling the "Be careful what you wish for" because all I could think was that I wanted Miranda more than ever.

It was also obvious one of the stagehands was hitting on her. "Cover me," I told Ryan. Fuck this guy. It was my job to keep Miranda, who was acting as pop star Lola Brandy's body double, safe. We had been hired to watch over primarily Lola, who was currently on stage, but also her team, which included dancers, the body double, and Lola's mother.

I relished the excuse to approach Miranda, make myself known to her.

The woman I had wanted with a lustful, blooming intensity since the age of fifteen.

The woman I couldn't have.

My brother's girlfriend.

"Is everything okay?" I asked, stepping into the guy's personal space. He automatically took a step back and it made me smile. Little douchebag.

"Yeah, why?" he asked, defensive. He was thin, wiry, smarmy. He looked guilty, darting his gaze around, avoiding my scrutiny.

When I turned to Miranda, I gave her a wink. "Ms. Bartello, you okay?"

She gave a gasp of surprise. "Alejandro! Oh my gosh, I didn't know you were here!" A smile lit up her features and I felt it all over again.

Desire. Lust. And something deeper.

Everything I'd felt all those years ago when I had fallen head over ass for Miranda the day I'd met her.

When my brother brought her home.

"I ask for all the jobs where I get to see sexy women."

She reached out and smacked my chest. "Why does that not surprise me? You're always such a ladies' man." Then she opened her arms. "Come here, give me a hug."

Gladly. I pulled her in to my arms and gave her a firm embrace, indulging in a sniff of her hair, her skin, her perfume. Her full breasts pressed against my chest and I wanted to turn, push her against the wall, slide aside her bodysuit, and make her mine. I'd take the hug for now. She broke the embrace and glanced backward at the stage.

The crowd was screaming their approval.

"Almost over," she said. Then she frowned when she realized the stagehand was still standing next to us.

"Get out of here," I told him, voice firm, grin on my face.

My talent is sounding and looking like I'm calm, I'm cool, I'm charming. But you know, don't fucking mess with me. The guy caught on to my real message and took off fast, walking down the steps to retreat into the interior hallway of the venue.

"Thanks," she said. "He was a little persistent."

I almost asked her why Max hadn't taught her how to knee an obnoxious guy in the nuts, but the last thing in the world I wanted to do was bring up my asshole of a brother. He was already an invisible audience, a palpable wedge between us. "If you want, I can go kick his ass."

She laughed and it was a sound that made my gut tighten. I had thought it would go away—this deep grinding need for her. But my adolescent desire had given way to something even more elemental, almost overpowering. I was in trouble. Or heaven, really. I was on more solid ground at twenty-five than I had been at fifteen, more confident. I knew myself. But I also knew Miranda still saw me as the little brother and I hated that.

"No ass kicking necessary." She touched my arm. "I have to go, but let's talk. I want to catch up and I want to ask you something."

Anything. She could ask me to walk naked over the causeway and I wouldn't hesitate. "Sure."

"I was planning to call you tomorrow actually."

Interesting. I couldn't imagine what she would want to talk about other than Max and I didn't want to talk about his dumb ass.

Lola came rushing off stage, her outfit identical to Miranda's. She tore off her mic and shook back her hair.

"That's my cue," Miranda said. "Gotta go." She gave me a wave and took the coat and sunglasses an assistant handed to her.

Lola had a personal bodyguard, and he was already whisking

her down the steps that led to the private underground passage to the parking garage. She would be secreted out and Miranda would pretend to be secreted out, but just visibly enough that fans would assume she was Lola. It was a bait and switch a lot of the stars used to make an exit without paparazzi on their ass. Lola got the beefy bodyguard. Miranda got a twiggy personal assistant.

"I guess you know her?" Ryan asked, coming up behind me.

Not as well as I would like. "You could say that."

Miranda was already ten feet away from me but I couldn't stop staring at her. I wanted to watch her body, her hips, her ass, her waist, sashay away from me in those sky-high heels as she raised her arm and slid the sunglasses on with a brief backwards glance at me. I wanted to think for just one sexy little second that she was my woman. All mine.

I saw the guy before Miranda did, but a split second after Ryan.

Most likely because I was in a haze of hot need.

Sex makes you stupid. Wanting sex makes you a downright moron.

Ryan said, "Eleven o'clock, move," and started stepping forward right as I saw him.

A big guy. Not muscular, but thick, beefy, with a stomach that required his belt be worn beneath it. He was moving slow and reaching for Miranda. He was kind of diving toward her, his arms flailing. It was not a graceful or professional move, but he was sweaty and determined, and looked crazy as hell. I moved, going straight for Miranda. Ryan would handle the guy.

The fat fuck collided with Miranda right as I got there, knocking her to the left, stumbling in her heels. A startled cry erupted from her mouth and I cursed my being distracted even for such a brief second. I grabbed her by the waist and swept her up into my arms before she crashed to the floor. "You okay?" I asked as I backed her away from the scene. I moved fast, wanting her away from any further danger.

Ryan had the guy on the ground and Lola's security team had also appeared, along with two other guys who were with our firm, and a couple of Miami Beach police officers. The response was admirable. Swift and sure from all angles. I carried Miranda down into what I knew was the dressing room area. I took her into the first room that was empty on the left.

"Where are we going?" she asked. "I have to go, follow the plan. I need to do my job!"

I held her tighter as she struggled to wiggle out of my arms. "Hey, slow down a second. I'll take you where you're supposed to go. I just want to know you're okay."

The guy didn't appear to have a weapon so he hadn't been a genuine threat but I was grateful for the asshole. I had Miranda in my arms for the first time ever, aside from the usual brotherly hugs. Sure, she was wiggling and distressed, but damn, those curves. So juicy, so firm, so… forbidden.

Her ass bumped my cock.

I stifled a groan.

She went instantly still, her shoulders stiffening. She turned and stared in to my eyes. "Oh my gosh, I'm sorry. I didn't mean to make this hard."

Then she realized what she had said and her cheeks went pink. I couldn't see her eyes behind the sunglasses. I bit my lip, but the laugh escaped nonetheless. "You did make this hard. Very hard." I couldn't help myself.

Miranda cleared her throat. "Put me down, you goof."

"I'm just doing my job, Mandy." But I did relax my hold on her, and carefully set her down. "How's your ankle?"

She winced a little, but put her full weight on it. "I'm fine, thanks." She licked her lips, a quick swipe of her pink tongue over her plump bottom lip. It was painted with a neutral lipstick or lip gloss or whichever of the two was the one that made a woman's lips shiny and sticky, with a hint of turpentine scent. Shellac, that's what it should be called. It wouldn't stop me from kissing her though if she would let me. But she would probably kick me in the dick if I even tried.

She saw me as Max's little brother, nothing more.

But Max was gone and everything was different now.

That didn't mean jack shit though. Nothing was different to Miranda.

"We have to go," she said. "Can you escort me to the hotel with my driver? I don't need any more delays. Geez, I think every other show someone tries to rush me thinking I'm Lola. Which is the whole reason I'm here of course. But that guy was huge and could have squished me." She smiled. "Like a pancake."

To give her props, she didn't look scared. Though it didn't thrill me to hear this was a regular occurrence. But of course it was. Fans were always wanting to touch their favorite star. Again, that's why she had her job. Miranda was trained in self-defense. I knew that because I had poked into her business over the years. I told myself I was just looking out for her but it was more than that.

"I need to clear it with Lola's team." I was still on the clock. "Let me make a call."

This was the downside of working for a legitimate firm. Channels of command and paperwork. I called my boss, who called Lola's team, who gave permission. It only took a minute, but Miranda was already impatiently looking into the hallway. I pulled her back. "Don't stick your head in the hallway."

She let out a deep huff of air, frustrated. "I have to go."

"What's the big deal? I talked to Lola's people."

Miranda crossed her arms over her ample chest. "This is my last night working for Lola. I want to end on a high note. Lola is throwing a little party for me later in the hotel and I just want everything to go smoothly."

"Did you get a new job?" I was distracted again by all that exposed skin. She was more fit now than she had been in the past. Years of dancing professionally had honed her muscles. Before she had been in shape from genetics, youth, and her love of dance. But now she was sculpted. A work of art resulting from healthy eating and a job that required huge amounts of training. I had no idea why she was walking away from Lola's tour, which was only halfway through its US run. It had always seemed like a job she loved.

"No. I'm retiring from dance. I'm thirty years old, you know. There are girls who are on this tour who are nineteen. I'm ready for something else, to live back in Miami again. Have a real home for the first time in a long time."

"You're back in Miami for good?" Interesting. The possibilities to charm Miranda into my bed would be endless. I felt a fissure of excitement. This was unexpected good news.

"Yep." She smiled brightly. "The plan is to go to culinary school. And have a baby."

What the fuck. That would be my jaw dropping and my dick shriveling. "You're pregnant?"

"Not yet." She licked her bottom lip and shifted on her feet. She looked nervous and a little shaky laugh confirmed that. "I don't have a boyfriend either in case you're wondering. I want to have a baby alone."

The door behind her flew open and a man with a headset was standing there. I wasn't even sure how to process what the hell Miranda was telling me. She wanted to have a baby alone? That seemed... exhausting. I love kids but shit, I wouldn't willingly want to raise one solo. Yet I was also totally relieved that she wasn't knocked up by some douchebag backup dancer or worse, an accountant.

"Miranda, car is waiting, let's go."

"Great, thanks, Bill." Miranda shot me a smile. "You coming?

You should join me for the party at the hotel. Hang out for a while. Maybe I can ask you that question."

"You can ask me now." She had my curiosity at an all-time high. What the fuck was even going on in Miranda's head? I had no idea. But I figured she couldn't shock me any more than she already had with the baby comment.

Wrong. I was totally wrong.

Once the guy disappeared from the doorway and we stepped into the hallway she said, "Okay. I want a baby, like I said. But what I would really like is to make a baby with you."

When I was a kid I took a baseball right in the eye. For a second, I felt nothing, heard nothing. It was like time paused and my vision and hearing disappeared. Then the shock of the pain came racing in.

This felt like that. For a second, I couldn't even process what Miranda had said. Then the shock had me saying, "What the fuck did you just say?"

A baby? A baby. With me? She wanted to make a *baby* with me.

And just like that, I was hard as a fucking rock.

I HAD THOUGHT about how I would ask Alejandro for his sperm for months and never had I rehearsed saying it in the hallway of the arena with tons of people milling around. God, why did I just blurt that out like that with no warning?

A lot of people laugh when they're nervous. But I really laugh. Like cackling that I can't stop. I heard it coming from my mouth and my cheeks heated up. This was so important to me and here I was jacking it up from the start. But I hadn't expected to see Alejandro tonight. His presence had caught me off guard completely.

"Surprise!" I said, trying to lighten the mood but just coming across as manic. "I'm ready to be a mother and I don't want to wait around for a relationship that may never happen." Simple, right? Except I was asking him to get busy with a plastic cup and then disappear for the most part. I winced inwardly. This wasn't no big deal.

He didn't say anything. Not a word. He was frowning. I fought the urge to blather on and try to convince him, make him understand.

I forced myself to shut up and wait. He needed a second. This was quite a request, especially considering I hadn't seen him in over three years.

But Alejandro wasn't saying anything and Bill, Lola's head bodyguard, was getting impatient. He reappeared and frowned. "Let's go." He pointed me to the doorway that led down to the garage. I went, because I had to and the silence had drawn out long enough to be awkward. I glanced back to make sure Alejandro was following me. He was, in all his muscular sexy swagger.

Damn, Alejandro had grown up in the last few years. I had first met him when he was a teenager. He'd been quick with a grin and had plenty of youthful cockiness. He moved differently now, like a tiger. Confident, muscular, the ultimate alpha male. His grin now was more sensual and charming versus mischievous. I hadn't expected to be attracted to him, but holy shit, he had gotten so hot. I spent plenty of time around good-looking and built guys. There were half naked dancers around me on the daily. But Alejandro had something special. He was gorgeous and a hell of a lot of fun.

He was no doubt a chick magnet. And he knew it.

After opening the door to the car for me, Alejandro stood there while I climbed in, his foot tapping hard on the asphalt. He bent over, his head appearing in the doorframe, his nostrils flaring. "You asked me your question," he said. "Now I have one for you."

I stared up at him, my heart racing in my chest. I shivered from the air conditioning the driver had blasting in the luxury sedan. "Yes?"

"Why me?" he asked. "Think about your answer."

Before I could respond he slammed the door shut. He walked around the back of the car while I struggled to figure out what to say. I couldn't tell him the truth. That I wanted his sperm because he was Max's brother. That really, ultimately, I had always wanted a baby with Max, but couldn't because Max was dead. Or presumed dead. No one wanted to hear they were the next best thing. I also couldn't tell him that I often wondered how stupid it would have been if I had gotten pregnant with Max. That I regretted my naiveté. Which made me feel a deep crushing sense of guilt.

I had thought about this endlessly, how to answer the question that anyone would ask. That I knew Alejandro would ask. I owed him a decent answer. I was asking for an enormous gift.

All my rehearsed answers seemed stupid and trite. I tried to dry my damp palms on my bodysuit but you can't dry anything on sequins. When he slid into the back seat next to me and turned to stare at me expectantly I swallowed hard.

I ended up with the most simple and straight-forward answer. "Because I love you."

The corner of his mouth turned up. "Like a brother. You love me like a brother. And siblings don't have babies together."

He had a point. Alejandro and his parents had been a huge part of my life for years. They were family. "But this would be my baby, my responsibility. I'm just asking for you to… donate."

At that, I saw my driver glance at me in the rearview mirror. Shit, he was listening to every word. Awkward. But I was in this far, I had to keep going. Think about the ultimate goal—becoming a mother.

"So you want my sperm and then you don't want me involved at all?"

An edge had crept into his voice.

"I… want you to be as involved as you want to be. As a friend. Not a father." I needed to be clear on that point. I couldn't co-parent with Alejandro. That would be a minefield I wasn't prepared to navigate. "So will you help me?"

"I watch reality TV," he said, inexplicably.

"What?" I asked, startled. Out of all my scenarios I had played out, Alejandro either said yes or no. He didn't go off topic. "So?"

"On those shows they are always hiring surrogates and they become best friends and everybody squeals and shit when she's pregnant like it was a job promotion instead of an actual creation of a human being. Or a lesbian couple asks a guy friend for his sperm and he says yes in like two seconds."

I had a sinking feeling the longer he talked. "Okay."

The hotel was only around the corner. We were already pulling up in front.

"This isn't reality TV. I'm not giving you an answer right now. In a car. Three minutes after you tossed this at me."

Yep. He was angry at me. If you didn't know him, you wouldn't be able to tell. Alejandro didn't get sour or frown. He continued to smile. If anything, he smiled bigger, which was frightening as hell. I should have waited instead of blurting it out like that. I should have taken him to lunch like I had originally planned. Caught up on our lives first. Then said, "Hey, let's make a baby."

This was me though. I always got ahead of myself. I didn't think of it as impulse so much as enthusiasm. I got carried away. Max used to say I was like a perpetual five-year-old. Except he never said "perpetual." More like, "Mandy, you're like a fucking five-year-old. So damn cute."

Max hadn't had Alejandro's charm. He was more straight-forward. Brusque. Misunderstood. Or he had been. It was still hard for me to remember he was dead and I had to speak about him in the past tense.

"I understand," I told Alejandro. "Take all the time you need and ask me anything you want." I would go ahead with my appointments as planned to ramp up my fertility. When he was ready, I would be primed for egg extraction. And if he was never ready? I would go anonymous. It wasn't my preference, but I wanted a baby no matter what. My goal my whole life was to have a child and now I had a ton of money saved from years on the road. It was time.

The driver cleared his throat. "Miss, we're here."

He wanted us out of the car. "Great, thank you."

I reached for the handle of the door, but Alejandro grabbed my wrist and stopped me. I glanced over at him in question.

"Hey. I love you, too."

That made my heart swell. The last thing I wanted to do was destroy the remaining fragments of my relationship with Alejandro, and the Garcias. I reached out and cupped his cheek. "You're such a good boy. You always were."

He covered my hand with his and he held it tightly. "Not a boy. A man. A grown-ass man with a man's needs."

What did that mean? And why on earth had my nipples hardened? Of course I knew he was a man. But I was older than him. I just thought of him as Max's younger brother. "What does this man need?" I whispered.

It was a dangerous question.

His answer was a sly, lustful smile. His eyes were dark. His shoulders tense. "You. That's what I need."

Whatever the hell I thought he was going to say it wasn't that.

The door I was holding yanked open and I almost spilled out onto the driveway. Instantly, lightbulbs flashed. Instinct had me sliding the sunglasses back over my eyes.

Bill was there to catch me. There were people yelling for Lola. I was out of the car and being hustled into the hotel, the whole time wondering what exactly Alejandro needed me for.

Maybe I wasn't the only one who had a crazy question to ask.

CHAPTER 2

When Max and I were kids, I figured out by the age of five, when he was ten years old, that he was the real-life version of Dr. Jekyll and Mr. Hyde. Not everyone saw the different sides of Max because he was good at hiding the darker side of himself. But he was completely unguarded around me. So I was there when he knocked over a vase and blamed it on the dog, even as my dad smacked the poor unsuspecting mutt on the rump. I was there when Max was twelve and tripped a girl his own age at the playground and called her a whore as he flipped up her skirt. Or the time he used his slingshot in front of me to knock the neighbor's cat off the fence, laughing hysterically.

All cruel, as symptoms of a bully, but not necessarily psychotic.

But I was accidentally there years later when I walked in on him with another girl while he was dating Miranda. He had taken my iPod without permission and I stormed into his room to retrieve it. I was pissed off that he was stealing from me when I knew full well he was selling weed and wasn't paying rent to our parents. There they were, Max and a brunette fully naked, the girl riding him like she was on the pro rodeo circuit, fondling her own nipples. She did pause long enough in her groaning and squeezing to smile at me and give me a friendly wave. "Oh, hey," she said. "What's up?"

I ignored her. "What the hell are you doing?" I asked Max. "Does Miranda know you're fucking other girls?"

Max gave me the stare. The one that only myself and a handful of other people had seen. The one that said I could die and he would not give a shit. In fact, he would enjoy watching. "Get the hell out of here," he said. "Or I will shoot you."

His hand went into his nightstand drawer and I was already backing up. I knew he had a gun in there. And suddenly it was out and pointed at me. And I had seen enough in our lives to know the truth. He could shoot me without hesitation. I had no doubt about that. The girl let out a squeal.

"What are you doing?" she asked, trying to maneuver herself off his dick, her expression one of alarm.

The gun shifted from me to her. "Don't you dare stop fucking me," he said. "I don't like a dick tease."

She went completely still for a heartbeat. I regretted riling him. I should have said something later, when she was gone. But I was so pissed off for Miranda that I had broken the cardinal rule of life with Max—don't poke the guy with the weapon. "Max, leave her alone," I said quietly, trying to stay calm.

But now he ignored me. He was focused on the girl, who couldn't have been more than eighteen. "Are you a dick tease?" he asked her, his voice like steel.

She shook her head rapidly and settled back on him, her thighs spread on either side of his chest. She started to move, her face leeched of color, all pleasure gone. He relaxed a little, his arm dropping down slightly.

At fifteen, I didn't know what to do. He was twenty, bigger than me, muscular, and crazy. I couldn't rush him, knock the gun out of his hand. That would be a huge risk and it wasn't just me I would be jeopardizing. I knew he wouldn't kill the brunette intentionally. But if I intervened further, he might by accident. So I did what I had always done in life with Max—I backed out. But I stood in the hallway, watching around the doorframe, just to make sure nothing went south. I felt sick to my stomach, horrible, in agony for the girl. She was moving faster now, spurred on by his hand smacking the back of her curvy backside. Her yelp was one of fear, not pain, and certainly not pleasure. He still kept the gun pointed at her, and I knew that I had inadvertently given him a new form of torture pleasure. Sexual domination. Fear mixed with sex.

It was my fault.

The wait felt endless. Interminable. But finally he gave a grunt of satisfaction as I sat with a noxious pit in my gut. A minute later she came out of his room, tears streaming down her face, her clothes in a bundle in front of her nudity. When I locked gazes with her, she sucked in a breath and recoiled from me. She was halfway across the living room before she paused briefly to pull her shorts and top on with trembling fingers, not bothering with undergarments.

"Do you need a ride home?" I asked her, my offer small comfort but sprung from genuine compassion for her.

She just ran out of the front door.

I didn't know it at the time, of course, that my parents knew about Max's other side as well. Every time I tried to rat him out or complain about his behavior, they always shut me down. Acted like I was imagining it, or exaggerating. Eventually I stopped trying, never knowing that they had fretted and talked and wondered and ultimately had decided the key was to keep him calm, and sweep up any messes he made along the way.

We were the Garcias, a regular working class family living in South Miami, and we were harboring a sociopath.

And because we were all afraid to trigger Max, we ignored it.

And made it worse.

I watched Miranda repeatedly glance over at me, her smile warm, but uncertain. Lola Brandy's suite was immense, with a balcony that wrapped around three sides of the building, offering views of the Biscayne Bay and downtown Miami. I loved the skyline at night. There was magic in the lights of Miami, dancing over the inky blackness of the bay. I had no desire to ever leave my hometown. Everything I could ever want was here—sunshine, the beach, clubs, women, music, food, money.

And now Miranda was even back.

Asking me to give her a baby.

The suite was filled with laughter and cocktails. Not a jam-packed party, but a dozen or so people mingling and chatting and lounging on the white leather furniture. Someday white furniture will go out of style in Miami, but not today. It was still the perfect backdrop for the deep blue of the bay.

Lola had changed out of the sequin jumpsuit into pajamas, but not like the kind you'd grab at Walmart. These were satin and luxurious, displaying her cleavage, and giving the air of Old Hollywood. I didn't know much about her other than what you would hear when a musician was dropping a new album. Sound bites. But she seemed friendly and not pretentious.

I was nursing a beer and moving from group to group, talking, laughing, watching. It was one of my best skills—being social under any circumstances. I introduced myself, answered questions about being a bodyguard, flirted mindlessly with a backup dancer named Zoe who had hit on me. But all the while all I could think was that Miranda had punched a hole into my stable life and squeezed my heart and my dick simultaneously. Not a good fucking feeling.

Miranda made her way to me, still wearing the stage costume. I thought it was weird that there were no arrangements for her to change when Lola herself had clearly ditched the sequins. But in my business as a bodyguard I had spent plenty of time around rich people and a huge percentage of them did shit that made no sense to a regular Joe like me. Or a regular Alejandro. The thought made me smile.

"You okay?" she asked.

I knew what she was asking. If I was upset with her. But I wasn't going to address what she had sprung on me here at this pop star post-concert get together. "Of course. How are you?" I gave her a smile and gestured to her feet. "Aren't your dogs barking?"

She gave a little laugh. "I had forgotten how much you sound like my grandfather. No, my feet are fine. I'm used to dancing and walking in heels around the clock. But thank you. How is the beer?"

Miranda had retreated into polite. Fine by me for right now. My thoughts were swirling into dark and dangerous places and I didn't need to have an emotional scene go down here. "It's wet."

Like I wanted her to be. Wet and writhing in ecstasy beneath me. Open to me, physically and emotionally. Eyes glassy with desire. Heart full of love.

Oh yeah. Not a goddamn thing had changed in the three years since I had seen her last. I still craved Miranda with every inch of my oversexed body. Maybe I even wanted her more because now she was a woman and I was a fully-grown man and I knew, I just fucking knew, that if she could forget my dickhead brother had ever existed, I could satisfy her. Love her.

I drained my beer and set it down on the wet bar, with a harder slap than I meant to do. It drew the attention of Miranda, who looked alarmed, and Lola, who glanced up from the sofa.

"Miranda, bring your friend over here so I can meet him." She smiled and waved us over.

I didn't wait for Miranda's response, who seemed to hesitate, but strolled over to Lola. "Hi, I'm Alejandro. Thanks for letting me join the fun."

"Thanks for keeping us all so safe." She took a small sip of her champagne and winked. Still in full stage makeup, she was a lot of false eyelashes and bronzer. But you could see the natural beauty there in the high cheekbones and the amber-colored eyes. "Those are some guns you have there," she added, gesturing to my biceps.

"Fully loaded."

Lola laughed at my over-the-top answer. I was flirting and she knew it. Probably expected it. "Let me feel them. Take your jacket off."

Hey, I work out. Nothing wrong with a little appreciation for it. Besides, it wasn't like Miranda cared what I did or with who. She just wanted my sperm, not me. Was I pissed off about that? Hell yeah. It's a weird thing to have someone say they want to recreate your likeness in the form of an infant, but they don't actually want you.

I wanted a reaction from Miranda. Maybe just a little jealousy. So I stripped off my jacket and tossed it on the coffee table. "Shirt too?" I asked Lola.

"Of course not!" Miranda said. "This isn't Chippendales."

"Speak for yourself," Lola said. "If he's willing, I'm wanting."

I shrugged. "I don't mind. This is Miami. I've had stranger requests than this." I gave Miranda a side glance. She blushed.

"Then by all means, take your shirt off." Lola turned to another woman sitting on the sofa with her. "Chloe, maybe you should close your eyes. I'm not sure you can handle all this man chest."

Chloe, a brunette with cleavage I could lose myself in for days, snorted. "If I get scared, you can hold my hand."

I undid the buttons on my dress shirt matter-of-factly. I wasn't going to put on a show, but I wasn't going to be shy either. I was already picturing bragging to the guys about how the pop star Lola Brandy had wanted to see my muscles. They would give me shit for days, but at the same time they would be jealous as hell. There was something so damn satisfying about pissing my buddies off.

Once my shirt was all the way off and I draped it over the table, Lola clapped. "Bravo."

That made me grin. I liked that she wasn't a diva taking herself far too serious. She was just having fun post-show and I appreciated that. Part of me was aware I wasn't helping my cause with Miranda. I wasn't exactly showing her how much I wanted *her*. But I have a habit, ten years deep now, of pretending I don't give a shit about Miranda and me, and I cover those feelings up with flirting, fucking.

Casual as shit, that's me. It's also the world's biggest lie.

But if Max and I have anything in common it's that we're both amazing liars.

Lola reached out and slid her hand across my abs. "A little lower," I told her.

Her laugh was practiced, melodic. "Aren't you a bold one? I like it."

THIS WAS WHAT I got for being impulsive and not sticking to my original plan of asking Alejandro to lunch. I was standing there third-wheeling behind him as he bared his chest for my boss. I was mortified. Mostly by the fact that I felt things that I should not be feeling. I was used to his attention being on me. It wasn't exactly a huge secret that as a teenager he'd had a crush on me. So in the past, his flirting had been directed towards me, and what woman doesn't like a little harmless crush?

He'd been discreet when his brother was around, obviously, and never took it so far as to make me uncomfortable, but I knew. It was because he had watched me carefully and had opened doors for me and rushed to help me with a bag of groceries when I went over to the Garcias. He had liked me.

Now he just seemed unconcerned with my presence. He'd been talking to everyone in the suite but me. But I couldn't exactly complain, because hello, I had just put him on the spot in a major way. Also, I had never given him any encouragement or any reason to think I would be okay with him flirting with me. In fact, the one time he had gotten a little too close to me, I had snapped at him and put him on guard, offering a sincere apology. I couldn't exactly expect him to sit around and think about only me for a decade. That teen crush was in his rearview mirror apparently.

Ricky, a dancer who had been on tour with Lola for three years, sidled up to me, his eyebrows raised. "Girl, where did you find this guy?"

"We grew up together, so to speak. I dated his brother when I was younger." But I realized immediately I should have just said we were old friends, because now Ricky, a well-known gossip, seemed intrigued.

"So there is another one who looks like this? Are they single?"

"Straight," I told Ricky. "Sorry." I didn't want to go into details and the whole sob story and tell him Max was missing. That he had disappeared and was presumed dead. People alternated between horror and gruesome curiosity and I wasn't up for that. "As for being single, I can't speak for Alejandro."

Another thing I had intended to ask Alejandro before I blurted out I wanted his sperm. It wasn't exactly fair to ask for a sperm donation without consulting his partner, if he had a girlfriend. Not that he looked like he had a girlfriend, given that he was now allowing both Lola and Chloe to pet his chest, but I still needed to ask.

I could see why they were enamored of his body. I only had a view from behind and it was still a great one. His shoulders were broad and muscular. His back was rock solid. He had tattoos on his biceps. A cross. A skull. Those were new. This was all new. He hadn't looked like that as a teen, and I hadn't had this reaction to him in the past.

I felt… warm. In my cheeks. In my womb. In my inner thighs, which suddenly seemed really damn exposed in this piece of nothing bodysuit. I basically had two inches covering my pussy and I shifted in my heels, feeling suddenly like desire was shooting out from me like a laser beam.

Panicked, I clapped my thighs together and crossed my arms over my nipples. Thank the Lord for pasties. No one could see the taut buds that were betraying me without warning.

"Whoa," Chloe exclaimed. "I went too low there, I'm sorry. But holy shit, your biceps aren't the only thing that's huge."

Everyone laughed. Everyone but me. Alejandro had a big dick? Why didn't I know that? Hell, why *would* I know that? Did I want to know that? My body seemed to think so. Confused, I decided since this was my last night on tour, there was literally no reason why I couldn't have a drink. I took a glass of champagne off the wet bar and took a massive sip and tried to tell myself my feelings were the result of emotions running high. I wanted a baby desperately. My hormones were playing tricks on me in pursuit of conception.

"You know what they say—speak softly and carry a big dick," Alejandro said. "I let it do the talking for me."

Again, a swell of laughter rose up from the room. Glad everyone was having such a grand old time. Though it was a scene that wasn't unfamiliar. Life on tour was a party, filled with sexual innuendo and jokes. Only now, it was different. I felt left out.

Alejandro belonged to *me*.

Not sexually, but he was my friend, my past. And here he was stepping into my world and yet ignoring me.

Lola patted the spot on the sofa next to her. "Have a seat, Mr. Big Stuff."

Some pop stars put on a show of flirtation but draw the line at sleeping around on tour, not wanting entanglements, stalkers, unexpected pregnancies. I had been with Lola for two years, and on three different tours before hers. She was the only one who didn't give a rat's ass about playing it safe. She loved a good boy toy in her bed and I knew that look in her eye. She wanted Alejandro.

And she would get him. Because she was Lola Brandy and no single man was going to say no to a piece of pop star ass.

Normally I could give two shits who Lola had sex with. She was a beautiful, talented woman. Men wanted her. She was single and at the top of her game. I wasn't even jealous of her success. She worked her ass off and deserved it and treated her staff well.

But this? Her interest in Alejandro made my gut hurt. It was a weird mingling of my two worlds and I did not like it. Not one freaking bit.

Given that I had no right to feel anything at all, I decided it was time for me to go back to my own hotel room. It was my last night on the tour. The next day I was moving in with a friend for a few days, and then on to my own apartment. My first real apartment in years. That was a pleasant distraction.

A home. Just me and eventually a baby. It had been the focus of all my financial goals the last few years and here it was—the big moment. A total life change. That's why I was feeling strange. Touring with Lola had been my world ever since Max had disappeared. My distraction, my passion, my family.

They had replaced that aching hole in my heart after Max had disappeared.

It felt so emotional to be leaving them, but also to have Alejandro mingling with my friends. It was overwhelming and all I wanted to do was run. Down the hall and in to the future.

I drained my champagne. "I'm heading off to bed, everyone. Tomorrow is a big day for me." I smiled at Ricky and gave him a hug. "Crap, I'm going to miss you so much."

"You're going to bed this early?" Chloe asked, surprised. "I thought you'd go hard tonight."

"Well, I am thirty, you know," I teased, not wanting anyone to read my true emotions. "Old lady alert."

"Oh my God." Lola rose and opened her arms, her lips turned down in a pout. "What am I going to do without you? My favorite mirror."

That made me laugh. I was no dead ringer for Lola but close enough for subterfuge. She had been good to me as a boss and I would miss her enthusiasm and endless energy. "You've been awesome," I told her. "And the next time you roll through Miami I will have my culinary degree and I'll be fat and happy. I'll cook you an amazing dinner."

"Send me cookies. You know how I feel about baked goods."

It was her weakness, just like mine. "You got it."

Alejandro grabbed his shirt off the table and started to pull it on. "I'll walk you back to your room."

"Oh, no, I'm fine." Now why in the hell did I say *that*? Was I an idiot? Apparently. Because under no circumstances did I actually want him to say okay and stay behind and party.

"Don't be stubborn," he said. "I'm your bodyguard. Let me guard your body."

"Girl, if you say no, I'm going to put on a gold jumpsuit and pretend I'm you," Ricky said.

That would be interesting to see Ricky attempt to pull that off, but not tonight. Alejandro was standing with his shirt open and his ab muscles descended in a V into the waist of his dress pants. I didn't mean to but I glanced and saw precisely what Chloe had been talking about. Huge, indeed. I swallowed hard. "Fine, you can walk me to my room. Good night, everyone, love you all."

"Glad you're in good hands," Chloe called out gleefully.

"I like to think *very* capable hands," Alejandro said with a smile that must have caused many pairs of panties to drop over the years.

Damn good thing I was in a jumpsuit or I feared I might find my own panties on the floor. I fanned myself. Something I hadn't missed about being home in Miami? The damn heat. And I was not talking about the NBA team.

Wishing I had grabbed another glass of champagne, I started back to my hotel room.

CHAPTER 3

wasn't sure what would be better—Miranda in the jumpsuit or out of it. There was something so ridiculously hot about her walking around in a fucking skintight leotard with her cleavage busting out the top and her thighs deliciously naked. There was a peek of ass cheek hanging out as well and all I could think was that I wanted a lap dance. She knew how to move. I wanted all that attention turned on me.

She was carrying a bag that she dug into and removed a key, never glancing back at me. I had no clue what was going on in her head. Hell, I had no idea what was going on in mine. I just knew that my already complicated feelings for Miranda had gotten more so. I was intrigued by the idea of giving her what she wanted, a baby. Our baby. But at the same time I wasn't sure my DNA was the best bet, what with a brother who was a sociopath. I also didn't want to go jerk off in a medical office and have them shoot my sperm into Miranda with the turkey baster. There was nothing intimate about that.

Props to science for making it work for couples struggling with fertility, but that was not what I wanted with Miranda.

She dropped her key and bent over to retrieve it before I realized what was happening. Those long, trim legs. That tight, pert ass. That sexy blond hair that made me want to wrap it around my fingers and tug.

The bag swung forward and fell off of her shoulder from gravity as she bent over. The momentum slammed her purse into the door. "Shit," she said.

The items inside spilled on the floor and I squatted down to help her retrieve them. A lipstick, aspirin, her wallet. The usual. Her phone had fallen face down but when I picked it up it was lit, probably falling on its side and turning the screen on. Her screen showed a familiar face. I only saw it for a flash before it went dark again and I fought the urge to hit the button, to see that grinning bastard behind her passcode request.

Why the fuck did she still have a picture of Max on her phone screen? Where she had to glance at it a hundred times a day. That was not cool. Not cool at all. Nor was it healthy. Five years. What had he done to deserve her devotion for five fucking years? Nothing.

She snatched her phone from my hand. She was looking everywhere but at me.

"Hey. What is going on? For real?"

Finally she stopped avoiding my gaze and we locked eyes.

33

With a little sniff she whispered, "What do you mean?"

"I'm coming in your room and you're going to tell me why you are here, in Miami. Not the partial truth. The whole truth."

Her eyelashes dropped, veiling her amber eyes. She tried to laugh, but it was brittle. "Don't you want to go back to Lola? I think you could get lucky with a pop star if you take your shirt off again."

"I know that. But that wouldn't answer my questions about you." I reached out and tugged the end of her hair and gave her a smile. "Don't look so scared. You know I'm harmless." Unlike my brother. "You just totally caught me off guard tonight and I want to know what's up. The full story."

"There's no full story. I just want to be a mother. I'm sorry I sprung it on you the way I did." She stood back up and opened the door. "Why don't you think about it and call me in a few days?"

But I put my hand on the door. She wasn't getting off the hook that easy. I hadn't seen her in three years and she had dropped a bomb on me. "Miranda."

"What?" she asked, flustered.

"Talk to me." Maybe I was pushing. Maybe I should walk away. But the majority of my life I had learned that if I was persistent I could get what I wanted in the end.

That was probably the one thing my brother and I had in common. Then again, Max never tried to coax. He just took. That wasn't my style.

I may not have ever gotten Miranda, but then again, I'd never tried. This was my chance. She had opened the door and I was going to stroll right in. I could feel it—that persistent desire spiraling out of control. Every feeling I'd ever had, every fantasy about her, felt like it was within reach if I played this all right. But first, I had to get her talking again.

She sighed and stepped into her room. "Get in here. I'm not having a conversation in the hallway. I may have left the tour but I still don't want everyone knowing my business."

I nodded and followed her. My shirt was still unbuttoned and loose over my waistband. It was a little ridiculous given that I was also carrying a gun, but this was my life. Hell, this was Miami. Over-the-top. Miranda's room was small but still pretty damn glam to my eye. It was modern, lots of white on white on white, and the drapes were open. She didn't have a view of the water, but the downtown skyline, and I walked over to it, appreciating the view from the vantage point. "It looks like you get to travel in style on the tour," I said.

"Yeah, Lola has been good to her team. Usually I have a roommate but they gave me a solo room since I won't be here for the show tomorrow night." Miranda came up beside me and looked out the window. "I did miss Miami. There is nothing like it anywhere else. The lights are so beautiful," she murmured.

But I was watching her, taking in her profile. "You're beautiful."

She gave a startled soft laugh. "Oh geez. Thanks."

"It's true." I leaned against the wall, cramming my hands into my pockets so I refrained from touching her. "You know I've always thought that. You know I always had a thing for you."

I half expected her to deny it. To bluster and act shocked. But she nodded. "I know. But I also know that you've outgrown it."

Her statement sounded more like a question. I shook my head. "I haven't grown out of thinking you're beautiful."

I saw her visibly swallow. "Are you seeing anyone?"

"I see a lot of someones," I said truthfully. "But no one special and never for very long."

"And why is that?"

"I'm sharing the wealth." I gave her a smirk. "What about you? No boyfriend?"

"I wouldn't have asked you what I did if that were the case." Miranda went over to the bed and sat down. She reached down to undo her strapped-on heels. "I haven't really had time to date."

That made me frown. "Are you telling me you haven't dated since Max?" I knew the answer. She still had his damn picture on her phone.

She shook her head. "Not really. It's been hard to move on."

I stayed by the window. I wanted to appear casual even though I felt anything but. "Then maybe asking me to give you a baby isn't the best way to make that happen. I am his brother." Unfortunately. "Every time you look at a kid, you're going to think of me. And him."

Then it hit me. That was the point. This wasn't about me at all. It wasn't like she thought I was a nice guy and had good genes. She wanted Max, and I was the next best thing. Fuck me. My nostrils flared.

Miranda stood up and went over to the mirror to undo the clip on the top of her hair. She was avoiding looking at me. "Why does everyone think I'm supposed to hit the one-year mark and just be able to move on? Grief doesn't work that way." She threw down the clip and shook her hair loose.

"There's grief and then there's flat-out denial."

She was attempting to unzip her bodysuit but she was struggling to get the zipper down. Frustrated with that and me simultaneously, she huffed. "You don't have the right to tell me how I feel."

I crossed the room in three steps and put my large hands on her zipper and started to take it down. She jumped and tried to pull away but I stilled her by leaning close to her ear. "Let me help," I murmured. "And you're right, I don't. But I'm concerned about you. I've always been concerned about you."

The frustration, old and gnarled and nasty, rose again. What the fuck did she see in Max? Or really, why couldn't she see the truth? He was good at masking his rotten inner core. But he wasn't *that* good. Even the world's best liar and sociopath can't hide how narcissistic he is. It pissed me off that Miranda was just perfectly willing to overlook all of that. Had she never noticed that Max didn't do anything that wasn't self-serving? That every gift he gave her came at a price? It was either a manipulation, like he wanted a guys' weekend in Vegas without her, or some bullshit apology, ie "Sorry I used your car and left the tank empty and you were late to work."

This was my frustration my whole life with Max. No one ever saw. No one. I was a man alone on an island and everyone had thought I was jealous of my charismatic brother.

When I got the zipper halfway down her back, Miranda shivered and turned around. Her eyes were troubled. "I can get it the rest of the way. What do you want me to say, Alejandro? A new relationship hasn't come along for me so I decided it doesn't matter. I want to move on with my life and become a chef and a mother. I'm sorry if that isn't enough progress for you."

"It's like this zipper," I said, brushing my thumb along her bare skin, feeling the ridges of her spine. "You can do it by yourself, but you'll struggle some." I needed to think about this, but I needed her to think about something too. "I know you're a very capable woman, Miranda. And I know you'll be a great mother. But before we discuss this any further, I need to know if you can agree to two conditions."

Her expression was wary. "What conditions?"

She wasn't going to like either one. But I had my limits.

"That you at least admit that there is a possibility that Max left of his own free will."

Immediately her mouth opened and she was going to protest. "Stop. I don't want you to defend Max or tell me I'm full of shit. I just want you to think about it. Nothing is one hundred percent. You can't know with certainty that he was abducted or met with foul play any more than I can know that he wasn't." I was pretty damn sure though, but in the interest of fairness, I couldn't prove it. So I just wanted her to say that it was possible. That her blind faith in him might have been misplaced.

She didn't say anything. She just stared at me. "The other condition?"

This one might go over with even less enthusiasm. "I don't want to go into an office and donate my sperm. I want to do this the old-fashioned way. I want you to have sex with me."

ALREADY FURIOUS FROM Alejandro's implication that I was an idiot for believing in Max, his follow-up request shocked me speechless. "*What?* Why?"

"Because making a baby is intimate and if you love me as a person, or friend, or whatever you want to call it, it shouldn't be a big deal."

His muscles and body and personality were crowding my space. I felt hot and flustered. "This feels like blackmail." It did. But it also felt... arousing. I was breathing too hard and it wasn't just from anger, though I was angry. It was from desire. I was attracted to Alejandro, there was no denying it, even though it was so damn wrong.

He was sexy, he was built. He had a devilish smile and charm. I knew him too, had known him for a decade, so he felt familiar, easy to be around. But he was Max's brother. I couldn't get over that. Max's brother who didn't even understand why I loved Max.

That was obvious. Or why I felt guilty.

"It's not blackmail. You don't have to say yes. You can still have a baby with someone else."

"That makes it blackmail."

He just shook his head, and the bastard was smiling, the grin of a playboy who knows he'll get exactly what he wants. "No. That makes it payment."

My hand flew up to slap him before I even realized what I was doing. I'm not a woman who runs around hitting men. This was the first time ever, in fact. Yet I was just so furious and offended. "I'm not a hooker, I'm your sister-in-law."

His instincts were better than mine. He grabbed my hand and stopped my momentum before my palm made contact with his skin. "You never married Max. So you are *not* my sister in any way. And I never said you were a hooker. Don't put words in my mouth. I told you that I love you and I meant it."

Confused, I stood there with his hand wrapped around my wrist. "But I don't understand why you would want this." For some insane reason I couldn't bring myself to say sex out loud, which was irritating as hell. I was thirty damn years old and I had toured with some of the biggest names in the music business. I had fended off creepers and stalkers and stage hands. I had endured endless days and nights on the road. I am not wimpy. Yet I couldn't say sex out loud. It was so stupid.

"Why do I want this?" he asked, startling me by running his finger down my back. "Or why I want this?" His hand drew across my waist. "Or this?" His voice was slow, seductive, his touch light as a feather.

I shivered as his hand rose near my cleavage without actually touching me. It was just a subtle gesture, an indication of his desire.

"Or why do I want these lips?" There was the pad of his thumb, rubbing across my plump bottom lip.

My anger mingled with confusion, which warred with desire. I wanted to touch his bare chest, to tilt my head, raising my lips to him. To peel down the bodysuit and stand before him naked, a full complete woman, with nipples begging for his touch. Not usually at a loss for words, I stood there, waiting. Needing. I had known him for a decade, but never like this.

"Do you really want to know?" he asked, bending down. He was so close to me I could smell his aftershave.

See the scar on his cheek that he hadn't had before. "Yes," I whispered. "I want to know."

"Because ever since I was fifteen I have thought you were the perfect woman and just once, I want to feel your skin against mine. That's all I've ever wanted."

Then he lowered his head and I knew what he was going to do. He was going to kiss me. And for whatever insane reason I was going to let him. His hand had shifted to cup my cheek with the softest touch imaginable. He had calluses and large encapsulating fingers, a big man with an even larger intensity. I had always felt older, wiser, and totally in control with Alejandro. It was because I was the first without dispute, the second in my mind because of the first, and the third because I had known he had that harmless little crush.

Now I was still older but that was it. I was not wiser, clearly, or I wouldn't be in a partially unzipped bodysuit. As for being in control? Not even close.

When his lips brushed mine I shivered. It went from the roots of my hair down my cheeks, over my shoulders, and rolled down the length of me. I sighed. I leaned. I ached. It had been a long time since I had kissed a man and this was different anyway. That had been an aggressive, let's do this, kind of a moment. This was hushed, anticipatory, a soft, sensual whisper. It was silk on my skin.

His lips took mine fully then, with a skill that left me flushed, reaching out for his chest, to hold myself up. He kissed like it was art and I was his canvas. But less studied. A self-trained artist who was worshipping me with his touch. Oh God, everything in me went still, hushed. Then passion rose, exploded inside me, his tongue teasing my lips apart and sliding past them. If he could do this, so easily draw desire from the depths of my core with just some kisses, what else could he do?

I was losing myself, drowning, digging my nails into his chest. Then he pulled away.

Leaving me breathing hard and leaning in to him, unable to think. At some point one of my shoulder straps had slipped off and I felt exposed, but I didn't make any move to cover up. I didn't want to hide from him. Alejandro was the one who reached out and slid my strap back into place.

We stared at each other for a few seconds, my heart pounding, breathing ragged in the quiet room. His eyes were dark, intense.

Then he leaned forward, breaking the moment, and he kissed my forehead. It wasn't sexual at all, and I was disappointed.

"Get some sleep. Think about it," he said. "Call me if you need help moving into your new place. I still have the same number." He stepped back and buttoned up his shirt. "And I'm good for heavy lifting."

Swallowing hard, I forced myself to nod. "Okay. Thanks. I have the same number too." How could he be so casual? I felt way off-kilter. None of this had gone according to plan. I wasn't supposed to be standing there speechless with tight nipples and a deep ache between my thighs.

Alejandro gave me a smile. "Good to see you, Miranda. I'm glad you're home."

I still couldn't think of a damn thing to say. But as he turned and went towards the door, I found my voice again. He wasn't going to come in here, turn my plan on its head, and then stroll out with a flip of his wrist in a very chill wave.

"Why haven't you texted or called me in three years?" I asked. That had been the last time I was in town and I had gone to see his parents and he had still been living with them. He had been aloof then, though still friendly. But he had said we should stay in touch and I had believed him. I had wanted to both believe him and have him in my life.

He stopped and turned, shaking his head. "Because it had to

be you reaching out. Because of Max. You had to come to me."

I don't know what I was expecting. Something that would put me back in control? I was the one who had rocked the foundation of our relationship and he was running with it. I couldn't put the genie back in the bottle. "I think we want two different things."

But he shook his head. "I don't think that's true at all. Sweet dreams."

He left my hotel room and I stood there, breathing hard, unsure what the hell had just happened. I went and took a shower and massaged my aching body under the hot stream. And damn it. I pictured Alejandro naked, in the shower with me, as I let the spray hit my sensitive flesh, my fingers teasing myself open, stroking.

It shocked the hell out of me that I came with his face dancing before my closed eyelids.

Oh dammit, I was in serious trouble here. Maybe we didn't want different things after all.

Because I couldn't deny that I wanted him.

Which was really freaking messed up.

Two brothers, two totally different personalities. And yet for all Alejandro made me feel unnerved, at the same time I felt very safe with him.

Safe, and very, very sexy.

And I came for the second time, this time his name on my lips.

CHAPTER
4

After a night of absolutely no fucking sleep whatsoever I sat across from my boss, Mickey Harris, bleary-eyed and unable to focus. All I could think about was Miranda. But she was why I was meeting with him anyway. I just wished I could get the image of her eyes, wide with desire, out of my head. Fuck, she had felt so good in my arms. Had tasted like everything I had ever wanted.

That kiss was ten years in the making and it did not disappoint.

Determined to focus on getting what I wanted, I cleared my throat and put the proper deference into my voice. "I want your help finding my brother," I told Mickey. "I know you have a lot of contacts. If he's out there, alive, I want to know where he is and what he's doing."

"I did know you have a brother even if this is the first time you've ever mentioned him," Mickey said, tossing his phone onto the desk and sitting back in his office chair. "And I knew he went missing. I did a background check on you when I hired you obviously. But the police didn't seem to think it was suspicious. It's just an open missing persons case, not an active investigation."

He wasn't telling me anything I didn't know. "I personally always thought he left on his own. Max wasn't always... concerned about other people's feelings, you know what I'm saying?" He was a prick. A well-masked prick.

Mickey nodded. "Yeah. Sort of like my ex-wife. Ryan's mother."

It was no secret Ryan's mother had taken off when he was a kid. I knew Mickey kept tabs on her. He liked to be ahead of his enemies, so to speak.

"Totally. But his girlfriend at the time thought he was abducted." Part of me understood Miranda's loyalty and respected it. But at the same time, it infuriated me. What had Max done to deserve such blind trust? It was the story of my life—people believed him and never saw the rotten core.

"Why, because she couldn't believe he'd leave her?" Mickey snorted. "Welcome to the club of every spouse ever cheated on or abandoned."

Exactly. But I needed to keep my emotions in check. If Mickey knew my real motivation he might not be so quick to help. "Basically everything that the cops said was evidence of him fleeing she thought was an indication of foul play. He withdrew forty grand from the bank two days before. Cops figured that was seed money to start a new life, but Miranda insisted he had been planning to buy a boat, and why would he leave without doing that? Also, she said someone might have known about the money and killed him for it. That he probably told friends he was paying cash for the boat."

"I mean, that is possible. Did he have a big mouth?"

"A huge mouth. Max was a bragger." I shrugged. "But his cell phone was found at home. Like he left it there. I think on purpose. She thinks it meant he was forced to leave at gunpoint."

"Any sign of a struggle?"

"No." Max and Miranda hadn't been technically living together. She stayed with Max when she wasn't touring. Once she had told me how much she appreciated Max not being a jerk about her job and how frequently she was gone. He had been standing behind her grinning. I knew he loved her traveling. It gave him free range to do whatever the fuck he felt like, and that included other women. She hadn't been anywhere near the apartment when he disappeared. "Max was living alone at the time but he had a lot of people in and out of that apartment and he wasn't a slob, but he was no neat freak either. There was clutter, but nothing abnormal like blood or tossed furniture."

Mickey nodded. "What was his favorite thing to do? He liked to go out on the water?"

"Yes. He did always want a boat, that's true."

"For sport or for fishing?"

"Speed boat."

"So he's probably not hiding in the Keys running a tour or

anything like that."

I tried to visualize Max in the laidback Keys and couldn't. "I doubt it."

"All right, well just give me everything you've got and we'll get someone working on it." Mickey was dressed casual in a T-shirt and khaki shorts, looking more like he was going fishing himself than running a multi-million-dollar security company. Despite his nonchalance as he rocked back and forth in his swivel chair, his eyes were shrewd. Mickey had seen a lot and was always suspicious of everyone, including me right now. "So what's the real reason you want to find your brother? What's changed?"

I could lie. But I wasn't a particularly good liar. I was charming sure, but that didn't work on guys like Mickey. My style was straight-out honesty. "Because personally I think my brother is a sociopath and I want to prove it to his ex-girlfriend."

It was the truth but Mickey saw through that. "And why is that? Why do you care at this point if she's hung up on him still?"

There was no way I was telling him about her request. But I could tell him how I felt. I had no interest in backing down from my emotions. "Because she should be mine."

That made Mickey grin. "Well, you know I'm a romantic guy. I'm all for love. I've been in love at least half a dozen times, and don't regret any of them."

It drove Ryan crazy that his father was a serial dater, but it made me like him even more. The guy liked women. I understood that. "Never regret anything you wanted at one point."

"You're a man after my own heart. So you nail that pop star the other night or what? I heard you were partying in her room."

Fortunately I hadn't, because I wasn't sure how happy my boss would be to know he had paid me to fuck someone. Not that Lola would have been the first time. But once I had seen Miranda, any other women that night were a no-go, even a pop star. "Nope. Miranda distracted me. I hadn't seen her in awhile."

Mickey held up his hand. "I don't need details, I'll just get jealous."

"It wasn't like that," I told him, which was a fucking shame. But I was working on it. "I thought you have a girlfriend now anyway, so what are you talking about?"

"Kim's pissed at me. She moved back out again."

Given that it was April and I was pretty sure she had moved in with Mickey during the winter, that had gone south quick. "Well, shit. That's no good."

He shrugged. "She'll come back. We like it this way. It keeps things spicy."

I couldn't even imagine a turbulent relationship like that. It was why I was never in one. I wanted uncomplicated. I wanted the flirt, the chase, the fuck. The walking away. Hitting the reset button and starting the process all over again. Fun without entanglements.

The only exception to that rule ever was Miranda.

"Whatever works for you, man."

"So give me a few days on this. We'll see what we can find out about your brother. If he's alive, we'll find him. There is no such thing as off the grid in today's world. I don't care how fucking smart you think you are."

Max thought he was pretty damn smart.

But it was time for my brother to stop being a pussy and come out and play with me.

THE LAST TIME I saw Max I had cried over leaving him to go on tour. I was going to be gone for eight weeks and it felt like years of separation. I wasn't used to touring yet. Max had smiled and tweaked my nose and told me not to worry. That time would fly by.

In a sense it had. It had been five years now since that fateful tour and the phone calls I had made frantically looking for Max. I was no longer twenty-five and still immature for my age. At the time I started touring, I had never been anywhere outside of Miami without my family and I hadn't left Max's side since we had started dating. I was sheltered and naïve in the beginning.

Not any more.

Not even after a year into my relationship with Max.

He had a way of doing that—of drawing people in, rattling their world, and sauntering off. I knew that. But he had never been that way with me. That was what frustrated me so much about everyone's opinions on Max and where he might be. No one knew that man like me. No one.

I sat across from my best friend from high school, Zoe. We

were at her parents' house because they had a pool. In high school I had spent hours and hours here. Before I met Max and found out just how much I loved being his sidekick, enjoying his attention and protection.

"So you legitimately just asked Alejandro to give you a baby." She was staring at me like she couldn't believe I had actually gone through with it.

I nodded. "Yes. Only I screwed up. I just blurted it out without any warning or prep or anything and he turned the tables on me, Zo. Big time."

Her mother had laid a brunch spread out for us and Zoe popped a grape in her mouth. "How? I mean, it's kind of a yes or no question, right? Take my sperm or hell no, you can't have my sperm."

Except there was a third option. One that made me feel warm from more than the South Florida sunshine. "He said he'll only help me out if we actually do it. Sex." Just in case that wasn't clear. "Like make a baby the old-fashioned way."

Zoe stared at me. "Hello." She was tan with dark hair that she kept pin straight. I had always envied that her skin tone allowed her to wear virtually any color or pattern. Today she had on a yellow bikini and she looked relaxed, confident, at ease.

One of the best things about coming back to Miami was going to be that we could hang out in person again. She had a boyfriend but they were still new-ish in their relationship and weren't spending every waking moment together.

"So are you going to boom boom with Alejandro?" she asked, raising her eyebrows up and down.

She wasn't acting as outraged as I had expected her to. "You don't think it's weird that he asked that? I mean, it's not really appropriate."

"Don't be a prude. You're asking him essentially a huge favor. Hey, let's make a baby, but then you stay the fuck out of it. I don't blame him for at least wanting to get off in the process."

At moments like this, I always felt like I'd been born in the wrong decade. I was pretty sure that I was supposed to be a 1940s chorus girl who went home to her midcentury modern home and cooked dinner for her delightfully charming husband, who wore a skinny tie. I was a woman who liked to be in a relationship. I wanted equality for women, for sure, but with feminism came the right to choose the life I wanted—and that was to be a veritable domestic goddess. I didn't want to hit the party scene and hook up with guys on dating apps. It just wasn't me.

And I didn't want to have sex with Alejandro just to give him five minutes of pleasure in return for something as amazing as giving me a child. That was not a fair exchange and it felt trite. Cheap.

"Any woman can get him off. He doesn't need me to get laid. Have you seen him lately?" I asked her, adjusting my chiffon cover-up printed with pineapples. "He's hot. He's built. And he can have any woman he wants."

"Sure. I saw him like six months ago in the Grove at a bar. He is super hot and yes, women were falling all over him."

I wasn't sure I really wanted her to confirm it for me. I shoved a piece of bacon in my mouth and chewed. "Exactly."

"But apparently he wants you. Which is intriguing."

"It's actually really terrifying." It was. "Because I don't know what to do. I don't want to make him angry so that he won't help me." But I wasn't sure I could have sex with him and not get emotional or feel weird about it.

"If he gets angry that you don't want his dick in you to create a baby then he can go fuck himself. Sperm is everywhere. Every guy has *millions*. It's not like his is so damn special."

Actually it was. Sometimes when I least expected it grief kicked me in the gut. I had gone to therapy. I had moved on, in theory. But I still missed Max and the messy connection we had had. I couldn't help it. And Alejandro was my last connection to Max.

"Oh no," Zoe said. "No, no, no. Don't do that. Don't get all weepy and googly-eyed over Max. It's been five years, Mandy. He doesn't deserve you sitting around doing Hail Marys and shit."

"Hail Marys and shit?" I asked, annoyed. "Do you want me to go tell your mother what you just said?"

For half a second she looked terrified. But then she relaxed. "She's at Publix. You can't tell her anything. Because you wouldn't do me like that, would you? My mom is fucking scary, you know that."

She was. That's why it was a valid threat. "I still could, you know, if you don't stop telling me that I'm an idiot for still caring about my boyfriend who disappeared under mysterious circumstances." Everyone seemed to forget that little fact. "Let's see how you would feel living in limbo."

Zoe chewed her lip and despite her wearing sunglasses, I could see she was mentally debating with herself whether she should argue with me or not. I knew full well she thought that if Max had been killed his body would have turned up by now. But we lived in South Florida. It took about a minute for a body to disintegrate. I had thought about it a million times. Visualized it. Kept myself awake at night imagining all the horrible things that might have been done to Max.

"I wouldn't like living in limbo at all," she finally said. "But I love you, Mandy, and I don't want you to be making decisions for the rest of your life based on what may or may not have happened to Max. If you want to make a baby with Alejandro, it should be because you think he would make a beautiful, kind, intelligent baby. Not because he's Max's brother. Because that's just holding you back in the past and not allowing you to move forward."

I sighed, frustrated. No one ever understood where I was coming from. "I am moving forward! That's why I am having a baby solo. I'm tired of waiting around to meet this mythical man I'm going to fall in love with and marry. He's not real." He was dead. That's what I really wanted to say. Max was dead. He had to be or he would have found a way to come home.

"Then just go to a sperm bank. You don't need Alejandro."

She was right. I didn't. It didn't matter. It was me holding on to the idea of what my future was supposed to be. I was stubborn though and not about to admit anything I didn't want to. "You want me to play Russian roulette with my child's DNA?"

Zoe just snorted. "Are you kidding? Everyone is playing Russian roulette with DNA. You don't know anything about Alejandro's background. People have all sorts of sneaky shit hiding in their genes. Cancer, diabetes, alcoholism, schizophrenia. You don't know unless you do a full screening."

She had a way of making me feel like I was hopelessly naïve. "That's reassuring, thanks."

"All I'm saying is love and reproduction are a gamble. You didn't even know Max as well as you thought you did."

My body stiffened. I was getting tired of her hinting about Max but never really coming out and saying what she was thinking. "What is that supposed to mean?"

"Oh my God," she murmured, lifting her sunglasses and rubbing the bridge of her nose. "I never wanted to do this. To have to say this."

Now she had me completely bewildered and more than a little annoyed. "What is going on?" I sipped my orange juice and made a face. It was going warm in the mid-morning heat. We were under an umbrella but that didn't mean anything other than the sun wasn't in my eyes. I wished it were. I wished that I was blinded and couldn't see Zoe because I had a really bad feeling that whatever was going to come out of her mouth was not going to make me happy.

"Max hit on me," she blurted out. "More than once."

I went completely still. I looked at her in shock. "What? Why would you say something like that?" Max was a flirt, just like Alejandro was. "Seriously, how dare you say that to me, now, after all these years? It's bullshit, Zo, and you know it."

Why did everyone want to take everything away from me? Why did everyone insist that I was a fucking fool? It made me furious. She was supposed to be my best friend and here she was telling me that for years she had allegedly kept a secret that my boyfriend had hit on her? I seethed, waiting for her answer.

"I'm not lying, Mandy, I swear. You know how there is harmless flirting and then there is, like, for real flirting? This was for real. He wanted me to go home with him when you were on tour." She pushed her breakfast plate away like she couldn't stand the sight of it. "God, my stomach hurts. I never wanted to tell you this."

"So why are you?" I felt like I was out of my body, like I had that day when Max didn't show up and no one could find him. When I got the phone call that he had missed Father's Day and no one had seen him in three days and I texted him a hundred times and called and asked around and nothing. No response and I had felt like I was watching it all from far away.

Now I felt like I did on stage, when the lights shone right in my eyes and I did everything based on muscle memory. It was an odd sensation, like being yanked back out of myself, the shadows and the light swapping out with each other until reality was hazy and nebulous. Zoe was breaking what remained of my old life. She was warping it and shattering it and making it all feel like a dream, like five years of my life had been a lie, when I knew they weren't.

"Because you won't admit that Max wasn't a perfect guy or a perfect boyfriend all the time. And if you won't admit that you won't be able to ever be with someone else because you're comparing them to an ideal that isn't even real."

I was hurt. I trusted Zoe to not be just another person who thought I was an idiot. "Nice to know my oldest friend thinks I'm living in a fantasy world." I pushed my chair back and stood up. "Thanks for brunch."

"Where are you going? Don't leave, come on."

"I'll talk to you later." I was too pissed off to stay and just splash around in the pool. That held zero appeal. "I need to go to the store. My moving day is tomorrow and I need towels and sheets." That was true, but mostly I wanted to get away from her.

"Miranda, wait." She stood up and started to follow me but I held my hand out to stop her. Rushing, I let myself out through the side gate and hurried to my car.

Once I was down the street, I pulled over and took a few deep breaths and tried to calm my shaking nerves. As angry as I was, I knew why everyone thought I was a moron. Because they didn't know what I knew.

They didn't know I knew everything about Max. Including his carefully thought-out plan to leave Miami and create a new identity.

The reason I knew he was dead was because he hadn't followed the plan. He hadn't contacted me the way we had pre-arranged.

But I couldn't tell the police any of that. So they didn't believe he had been in danger and that was why I went around and around in my head, the girl who can't leave the past alone. The past was murky and unresolved.

And Alejandro had answers I wanted.

He knew his brother better than anyone. Maybe even better than me.

It was true I wanted to have a baby desperately with him. But I also wanted to know what he knew.

My phone buzzed in my purse. Speak of the charming devil.

We need to talk.

We certainly did.

CHAPTER 5

Miranda had agreed to meet me to talk the day after her move. What she didn't realize was by "talk" I meant strip off our clothes and fuck all damn night. I'd explain that part once I was in her house.

She had brushed off my offer to help her move, but that didn't mean she didn't need assistance. It just meant she was stubborn as hell and unsure of what was going on between us. So I went to her new place anyway, despite her telling me not to after I had texted her, and found her standing in the driveway looking both flustered and sexy. She looked like old school Miami, when criminals and pinup girls ruled the beach. Her hair was big and blond, her sunglasses white and round, her top off the shoulder and tight. She was wearing sandals with heels and directing a two-man moving crew with lots of hand wringing and odd noises.

"Oh geez, I don't know. The living room?" she asked the one

guy who was standing there with a lamp in one hand and a box under the other arm. "Do you think it will fit?"

He just stared at her blankly and waited.

"Yes, the living room. I can move it later if I need to." She exhaled, the puff of air actually moving the hair on her forehead briefly.

I strolled up the drive, amused. "Moving sucks, doesn't it?" I asked her.

She looked at me, startled. "Oh, hey. What are you doing here? And I have no idea. I've never moved before. But I have to admit, this is a little overwhelming."

"That's why when people offer to help you, you say yes." I leaned over and kissed her briefly, before she would have time to pull away.

Her cheeks turned pink and she was so goddamn beautiful it hurt my heart.

"Lesson learned," she said breathlessly. "Thanks for coming by. You said we needed to talk anyway."

"That can wait. Tell me what you need me to do. I'm here to sweat on your behalf."

Her eyes widened. "Oh my. That is an offer I can't refuse."

She wasn't going to refuse any of my offers before we were done. Hell, if I had my way, we'd never be done. Miranda had come back into my life unexpectedly, but that wasn't surprising. Sooner or later it was likely she would have returned to Miami. What was far too tempting to pass up was that she had asked me for a baby.

To me, it was just a sign that we were meant to continue to know each other. To be something. Lovers, for sure. It was more than I had ever expected to have, and I was grabbing it by the fucking fists and holding on tight.

This was my fantasy, sprung to life. The moment when I got to play out all those thoughts that had rolled around in my teen head. Only it was going to be better, because it was real.

I wanted it to be as real as possible.

"Good," I told her. "I don't want you to refuse me."

She knew what I meant. She heard the double meaning. There was sexual tension zinging between us in the driveway. It was noon and we both were turned on. For me, it was a pleasant reminder of how amazing this was going to be. For her part, she looked equally turned on and terrified.

"I don't remember you being such a naughty boy," she murmured.

"You just weren't paying attention." I winked at her. "Besides, if you haven't noticed I'm more man than boy now."

Miranda rolled her eyes. The movers came back out of the house and went into the truck. They were lifting out a sofa.

"Where did all this furniture come from?" I asked.

"My parents. They sold their house and downsized to a condo in Broward. They bought all new stuff and gave me the old, which is awesome, because obviously I have nothing." She pressed her hands to her cheeks. "I can't believe this is actually my place. This is so cool and amazing."

"It's a cute house. Can you give me a tour?"

"Sure. I mean, it's just a rental, but I'm planning to be here at least two to three years. I'll be done with school in two." She started towards the house.

It was a squat midcentury style painted a peach color. It was actually a duplex, the house attached to a mirror image. Both had turquoise doors. The neighbor's stoop had yellow pots with flowers in it and two yellow rocking chairs on the patchy grass. I liked to see they were taking care of their half. It was a good indicator of decent neighbors.

"Where are you going to school?"

"Miami-Dade, the downtown campus. I chose this neighborhood because it's reasonably close, yet you know it's safe around here."

"Yeah, but I'm going to check your locks just to make sure everything is secure." I was also going to make sure the movers thought I lived there too because I did not want these guys thinking a woman like Miranda was flying solo. How hard would it be for one of them to come back at two in the morning and break in if they realized she was a single woman and vulnerable? The thought made my blood turn to ice.

"I think they're decent, but sure, if it will make you feel better."

"It would. It's my job, after all."

Miranda paused in the doorway and glanced back at me. "How did you end up a bodyguard?" she asked. "That's not what you wanted to do."

She knew way back when I had wanted to be a teacher. That I had spent a year in community college studying with that goal in mind. "School wasn't for me," I lied, because it was the easiest answer. "I do coach a baseball team though. Ten-year-olds. I love it."

"I can picture you doing that. You're great with kids."

My eyebrows rose and I stared at her, waiting for her to realize what she had said.

She frowned. "Well, it's true. You have caring qualities, that's why I… want you."

Her discomfort was adorable and I couldn't help but tease her. "Want me for what? I have no idea what you're talking about."

Miranda surprised me though. She lifted her chin and said, "I want you to get me pregnant."

Right as the movers came up with the couch.

I grinned. That impressed me. She was not playing around here.

One shot me a sympathetic look. "First the house, then the baby, eh, amigo?"

"It looks that way. No harm in trying at least." I gave Miranda a wink before smiling at the mover.

"That's the best part. Trust me, I have three kids." The guy didn't look like he was straining to hold the couch but he did look like he wanted to get his job done. "Where do you want this?" he asked me.

"That's for the woman of the house to decide."

She gave me a look that indicated she knew precisely what I was doing.

"Where do you want it, baby?" I asked, keeping my voice neutral. Normally I would have turned that in to a suggestive comment but not now, not with her. She wouldn't want me to be dirty in front of strangers, and no matter how much I wanted Miranda, I respected her more.

It felt ridiculously natural to call Miranda a term of endearment. I hid it behind a smirk, because I was actually feeling fucked up, confused, and filled with longing. This little domestic scene should be real for Miranda and it wasn't. This was what I wanted for myself—a home, a family, an ordinary life—but then as I got older, I had crushed my own dreams intentionally. I had focused on keeping life light and fun so that I wouldn't be tempted to drag an innocent woman into our crazy family. But Miranda already knew what she was getting and it was an intriguing possibility—Miranda as mine.

In just a few days the earth had shifted. Possibilities had opened up. All with her appearance and a request that was anything but simple or small.

I had to play this right.

She was not going to be the one that got away or hell, the one I never got. Not anymore.

"Under the front window, thanks," she said to the mover.

We had retreated into the house to give them room to maneuver when Miranda shot me a glare. "They're going to think we're a couple and that you live here."

"Hey, you're the one who asked me to get you pregnant," I said, mildly.

She did not look amused. "I didn't realize he was standing there. This isn't a joke."

"My point precisely. Look, Miranda, it's better this way. Adult men should not know you live alone. It's dangerous."

We were murmuring in low voices in the kitchen.

For a second she looked like she was going to protest but then she just nodded. "That makes sense. I know you're right, and honestly, I didn't think about it before."

"That's what I'm here for. I aim to please."

"You aim to make me uncomfortable."

"That's not true. I want you comfortable. Very, very comfortable."

She leaned on the countertop, which was very retro. It was a faded yellow Formica. About to respond, she suddenly winced. "Ow, I just cut myself on the sink edge."

"Are you okay? Let me see." I moved over to her but she was already running her hand under the water.

"I'm fine." She waved me off.

"Damn, no one has touched this place in fifty years." It was like Lucille Ball might stroll through the door at any second. I turned the faucet off for her when she removed her hand. There was rust around the rim where the hardware met the countertop. "Everything is a little rickety in this place."

"I like it. It's homey."

That was her theme apparently. Miranda wanted to be home. To make a home. To create a space for herself and eventually a baby. I understood that. I had never felt like my house growing up was a safe place. There was always too much tension for it to be all Leave It To Beaver, Cuban style.

Crazy to think we had both wanted the same damn thing.

She had just picked the wrong Garcia brother.

For this size rental in a safe neighborhood, this was probably the best she could get since she was going back to school. "You're going to make it something special, I know. Like you."

She opened her mouth, but then quickly shut it again. "I'm going to try."

"What do you want me to do? Start unpacking some of these boxes?" There was at least six in the corner of the kitchen. "Or help the movers haul stuff in?"

"If you can help the movers that would cut down my time that I have to pay them." She gave me a smile. "Thanks. You're a good man."

Compliments make me uncomfortable so I waved it off. More to the point, I wasn't so sure I was a good man at the moment. Everything I was doing was pretty damn self-serving. Mostly, I was a man not above lifting a few boxes to get what I wanted. But I would do it for Miranda anyway.

I would do just about fucking anything for Miranda.

I peeled off my shirt and went to lift boxes in what someone might say was a pursuit of pussy. Hey, I couldn't argue it. I figured I wasn't the first man and I wouldn't be the last to do just that.

ALEJANDRO HAD STRIPPED his shirt off and was hauling furniture, my mattress, and boxes galore in the afternoon heat like it wasn't straining him at all. He was joking and laughing with the moving crew and looked like he didn't mind in the slightest that he was spending the afternoon in manual labor for me, his brother's ex-girlfriend. Or girlfriend. I never knew how to phrase that when people asked. Ex implied breakup and that wasn't the truth. But we hadn't been married so I wasn't a widow. It was complicated. Like everything.

Like my attraction to Alejandro. He looked amazing without a shirt. Like a male stripper in a Vegas show. Muscular and covered in a sheen of sweat. His shorts kept slipping down and he would pull them up, but not before I caught a glimpse of some rock-hard abs descending.

I stood in the window, watching him, and unwrapping juice glasses. It was taking me forever to stack them in the dishwasher because I kept glancing outside to check out Alejandro. My mother had mentioned repeatedly the glasses had been in storage for months and needed to be washed before using and I felt like if I took the lazy way out and just put them in the cabinet, I wouldn't be able to drink orange juice without guilt. My mother took no shortcuts when it came to her household. But I scrubbed and rinsed absently as I watched Alejandro come in and out.

Helping me and looking hot.

The question I kept asking myself was why? Why was he here? Why did he want to have sex with me?

The only answer I kept getting was that maybe that ancient crush was still in place. But that seemed so farfetched. He was a ladies' man. Everyone knew that. I was no troll, but I wasn't the hottest of the hot, either. I work out, sure, and spend a ridiculous amount of time and effort sculpting my ass, but a lot of women in Miami had butts to envy. It must be more like I was the forbidden fruit since I had been with Max. Alejandro wanted a bite.

That thought gave me a swift kick of desire. Right downtown. A warm ache took up residence and wouldn't go away. That kiss popped into my head and I gripped a glass so hard it almost shattered. I decided to screw the glasses and move on to the plates and I scrubbed and I rinsed and I got more and more turned on by the memory of that kiss and the idea that Alejandro could turn some of that charm on to satisfying me. Was he good in bed? Presumably. He certainly had enough experience if the rumors were true.

Chloe had mentioned he had a huge cock. I hadn't studied it, but I wanted to. I wasn't sure I knew what constituted a small versus large penis. I just didn't have knowledge of multiple dicks, which made me grin as I stood at the sink. Girlfriends would show me dick pics but it was just hard to grasp out of context. Maybe it didn't matter if he had a huge cock or not if he knew how to use it.

What would I do if Alejandro came up behind me, bent me over, and slid down my pants?

Would I feel guilty? Like it was a betrayal? Or would it just feel so damn good I didn't give a shit.

Without realizing it, I spread my legs a little, visualizing all his rock-solid muscles flexing in his back and arms as he slammed his cock into me, large hands gripping my hips. Yum. I wanted that. I couldn't deny it.

"The movers are done. They need you to sign their paperwork out front."

I jumped, startled out of my dirty fantasy by Alejandro speaking. "Oh geez, you scared me."

"What were you daydreaming about?" he asked. "Your cheeks are pink."

I bit my lip. "Things I have no business daydreaming about. Ever."

His eyes narrowed. "Tell me about it. I want to hear what you have no business thinking about."

I couldn't tell him I was thinking about him fucking me from behind over my sink. But I did have a question for him. "Why sex, Alejandro? Explain it to me."

He just went for a glass of water and wiped his forehead. "Go take care of the movers, Miranda."

His voice was casual. Yet it felt a little bossy. "Hey, don't tell me what to do. I'm still older than you."

"I thought you liked a dominant man. You were with my brother, after all."

That shocked me and pissed me off. I opened my mouth but I couldn't think of anything to say. He had a point. I stormed off and went to handle the moving bill. I smiled and signed the paperwork and said my thanks and the whole time I was trying to find the best words to put Alejandro in his place. What had he known about my relationship with Max? Max hadn't been abusive toward me at all. But he had been dominant. The middle child of three girls, I had craved the attention he gave me. At twenty years old having him tell me what to do had felt like affection, caring. He had nurtured me.

My mind was racing, trying to remember how Max and Alejandro had gotten along. It seemed to me that they had been close. No animosity.

"Your husband is the first guy I've seen who can keep up with us," the guy who had introduced himself as Javi said. "If he needs a job we're always hiring."

Annoyed with Alejandro, for forcing me to be honest about the past, yet grateful he had saved me some money by helping out, I gave a non-committal smile. "I'll let him know."

Alejandro came to the door, his shirt back on, and cheerfully waved to the guys. "*Gracias*, man, appreciate it."

"No problem. Take care of your beautiful wife." Javi gave me a wink. "Have a nice day and good luck with the baby making."

Annoyed with both of them I just rolled my eyes. "Thanks.

Why don't you tell my *husband* to stop putting conditions on my request and just give me a baby?"

Javi ripped the paper off his clipboard and handed me a receipt. He glanced over at Alejandro. "Did you ask for a boat first or something? Damn, I should have done that. I didn't even think to negotiate."

"I doubt I'll win this round," Alejandro said.

This wasn't a game. This wasn't cute. It wasn't a flirtation. This was my life. My future. My child.

I thanked the mover again and just pushed Alejandro back into the house. "Stop making a joke out of this," I said to him after he closed the door. I was furious. "And what is your problem with your brother? Why do I have to admit to you that maybe Max wasn't a perfect person? Which is stupid, I might add, because no one is perfect."

"Max was a dick," he said baldly. "A complete selfish, narcissistic asshole. And you're the only one who doesn't think so."

Whatever I had expected him to say, it wasn't that. I gasped. "Excuse me? What the hell are you talking about?"

Alejandro leaned against my front door and crossed his arms over his chest. "Max was a dick," he repeated. "He was a bully, a liar, manipulative, and shady as fuck. You have to know that. You can't possibly believe that he was a model citizen."

I was stunned. I had had no idea that Alejandro felt that way about Max. "So what does that make you? You always pretended to be cool with your brother. So are you a manipulative liar too?"

"I'm a peace keeper." He smiled and held his hands out. "I always have been. Always will be. I learned at an early age that Max was good at using people and fooling people and that I looked like a jealous younger brother if I said anything."

"Speaking of, yeah, you do." I was outraged. Max had been far from perfect, I knew that. He *was* manipulative and he had a cruel streak that surfaced when we fought. But he was a good, kind man who had loved me and his family. "Max cared about you."

But Alejandro just scoffed. "Max never cared about anything but himself. He was very good at playing the game."

That was just insulting. "So you think that he didn't care about me? That I'm just an idiot?" God, it was like everything I had ever thought destroyed in just a few words. I was staring at Alejandro feeling like I didn't know him at all.

Zoe's accusation rose up in my mind, ugly and unpleasant. A niggle of concern started deep inside me and began to pulse, refusing to let me ignore it.

"I think he cared about you," he said softly, his voice heavy with regret. "I'm not trying to hurt you, Miranda. I just need you to understand that if I do this, give you a child, one, you know I'm doing it for you. Because this is what you want. And two, that you realize it won't be a recreation of Max. It will be my child, and ultimately Max and I are nothing alike."

I didn't think of myself as someone who has nothing to say but Alejandro kept rendering me speechless. I realized I had made a mistake. That I hadn't known him well in the years since Max had gone missing. Either Alejandro had changed or I had done a poor job of assessing his feelings back when he was a teenager. "This isn't how I expected this to play out, I have to admit. Just forget I asked. Thanks for helping me move." Now leave. That's what I was thinking. Just get the fuck out of my house and stop insulting me.

"You're welcome." He didn't move. He just watched me.

My cheeks felt hot from anger. His stare had me flustered. "It's nice to see you. Let's just start over on the right foot again. Forget I mentioned the whole baby thing. I don't want to argue with you."

It was a personality trait or flaw, some might say. I didn't like to argue or fight with anyone. Just like that, I reversed and essentially apologized. I realized I had always done that with Max too. Max had taken advantage of it, I could admit that.

But Alejandro just shook his head. "We're not arguing. I'm just communicating with you. Just making sure we are clear and on the same page. You couldn't have thought that I would just hand over sperm without some questions."

Maybe I had. I wasn't even sure now. But I had made a plan and Alejandro wasn't cooperating with it. "I didn't expect that you would attack the integrity of my relationship with Max." Damn, that sounded way more pompous than I had intended.

His eyebrows rose. "So you're telling me that you have no doubts about Max's perfection? That he was totally ethical, aboveboard, and never had a lie pass his lips in the entirety of the time you knew him?"

Guilt niggled at me. I couldn't say that. I knew full well Max had been engaged in illegal activity. But I couldn't betray him now. Nor was I going to admit that our relationship had flaws because it made me look stupid. "Of course I can't say that. Everyone lies at some point. But you are implying he was evil and that isn't true."

No one had seen Max take care of me when I got the flu. How he had held my hair back while I threw up and made sure I had fluids and changed my sweat-soaked T-shirt with tender hands. Evil people don't do those things.

What most people are is somewhere in between saint and Satan. They are shades of gray.

Look at me. I consider myself a decent person who wanted to cook and make a baby.

Yet I had been a drug dealer. An unintentional one, but a drug dealer nonetheless.

Not that Alejandro knew that.

But that was my point. He didn't know everything about Max and me.

But I guess that was his point, too. I didn't know everything about him and Max.

"Evil is a very dramatic word for it," he said. "I would say selfish and narcissistic, definitely, like I said." Alejandro gave me a smile. "I'm going to head out. Just think about it. I'll be around if you want to talk. Or if you want to make a baby."

It still didn't make sense to me, what he wanted. "If you don't have any love lost for your brother, then why would you be willing to help me?"

The smile turned sly, sensual. "Because I love you. My answer is the same as yours."

That wasn't reassuring at all. I just felt suspicious of him. It was an odd feeling in relation to Alejandro. "And on that note, goodnight, Alejandro."

He just laughed. He didn't try to convince me or explain himself further. "Goodnight, Miranda. Sleep tight."

I didn't think he would leave. But he just pulled open the door and started down the walk. His words reverberated in my confused brain.

Because I love you.

And suddenly I was going out the door after him. "Alejandro. Wait."

He turned immediately, his expression curious, but not casual. He might think he fooled other people with his casual charm, but I knew him better. I did. Maybe I didn't know everything. Hell, maybe I knew next to nothing. But I knew Alejandro had deep, loyal feelings for those he cared about. He stuck. He was a kind, caring man.

If he said he loved me, he did.

That right there was why I wanted him to be the father of my child.

My heart was racing and I opened my mind. I could lie and say I hadn't been lonely or that I hadn't missed the touch of a man who knew me, who genuinely cared about me. Hookups are not the same thing.

This wouldn't be a commitment, but it was a relationship. This would only expand on the connection we already had and would give us both exactly what we wanted.

"I…" For some reason the words got stuck in my throat.

God, he was right. I wanted a dominant man. I wanted him to tell me. I wanted him to take me.

He knew it too. The corner of his mouth turned up in to a slight smile and he started toward the house, stalking me. He stopped right in front of me. I stared up at him, waiting. Then his hands came up to cup my cheeks and he leaned down and kissed me—a hard, angry, demanding kiss, that made my insides tighten with need. Expertly his tongue swept open my lips so that he could dominate my mouth, while his hands wound up into my hair and twisted the strands.

It felt like drowning. Being dragged under by a riptide, and swept out to the open ocean. That had happened to me when I was about ten years old, being dragged under by a current, and feeling powerless, panicked, until it had spit me back out.

This was similar, but it was the desire, an intense overwhelming arousal that had me stunned, unable to free myself. It wasn't until he stepped back that I could even think.

"Get in the house, Miranda," he said, his voice low and rough.

I didn't even hesitate.

CHAPTER 6

couldn't have stopped myself from kissing Miranda for anything. The way she stood on her stoop, framed by the doorway of the house she was trying to make a home, dressed in those sexy shoes and tight pants, I had never wanted a woman as much as I did her.

The way she said my name—a plea—almost undid me. So I had kissed her and now she was obeying me by turning and retreating into the house. My cock was throbbing, my heart racing, and I felt the heightened anticipation of knowing I was going to get what I wanted—her.

I had always fantasized that I would take this slow, that I would be sweet and loving and tease her into full satisfaction.

But all these years of wanting her just caught ahold of me, gripped me in its fury, and I pushed her up against the bare wall in her entryway, kicking the door shut with my foot. Her eyes widened and she moistened her bottom lip.

Burying my head in her neck, I bit her earlobe, possessively, needing to get some of my feral energy out. She gasped in delight. Running my tongue over her sweet flesh, I found her pulse and sucked it for a second, closing my eyes to process that this was actually happening. I was tasting Miranda.

"What are you doing?" she asked, sounding scandalized.

Raising my head slightly, I slipped the front of her shirt down below her breasts. "Consuming you," I told her, lifting her breasts so that her nipples were closer to me, an offering. A meal. "You taste delicious."

With that I took her nipple into my mouth and sucked, teasing her with my tongue. Miranda gave a low moan that made my cock harden to steel. She was all juicy curves and soft skin. I wanted her naked. Now. But I'd settle for these bountiful breasts displayed for me with all their pink perfection. I bit her nipple, just a light nip, and that previous moan was nothing compared to what she gave me now. A rich cry of anxious desire, torn from deep inside her. Her hands gripped my shoulders, nails digging into the cotton of my shirt.

I wanted her to claw at my flesh. To rip my skin open and leave her mark on me. So I briefly stepped back while she gave a soft sob of disappointment. I raised my shirt over my head and tossed it on the tile floor.

Her hands reached out, eager to touch me. While her palms ran over my chest, my muscles, her eyes drifted half closed. "God, you're so hot," she said. "But I bet all the girls tell you that."

"I've only ever wanted to hear it from you." That wasn't a line. I didn't need the ego stroke of women telling me I was hot or had a great body. I worked out hard as hell. I knew what I looked like naked and it was pretty fucking good. But that I would hear those words roll off Miranda's plump kissable lips meant more than a thousand girls saying the same.

As she explored my body, I teased at her nipples with the pads of my thumbs, back and forth, back and forth, rolling the buds into tight peaks. Goose bumps rose on her flesh, and her breathing changed, grew short and anxious. Her reactions were priceless. Easy to coax forward. For a split second I worried that she hadn't been with anyone since Max, and how fucking weird that would be, but then I shoved that thought to the back of my head.

Max had given all this up.

She was mine now. All mine.

And if her lips tasted so damn good, her pussy would taste even better. I yanked on the waistband of her pants and the stretchy fabric gave in to me. After a few tugs I had them past her thighs, taking her panties down at the same time.

"What are you doing?" she asked, sounding both eager and frightened.

There were a million things I could say as I cupped her cheek and kissed her, not as dominating as before, my finger teasing across her clit, and finding her damp heat. I could tell her I was making her forget the past, or that I was making her mine. That I was giving her exactly what she wanted, whether she had realized it or not. I could tell her the hard and brutal truth.

Or I could just show her.

So after a few strokes, as she relaxed her grip slightly, I went down in a squat and I buried my tongue inside her core.

"Alejandro," she said. "Holy… shit."

The words were drawn out in an anguished ecstasy. "Yeah, baby?" I asked, before tasting her again, thoroughly. She tasted tangy and sweet and I couldn't get enough of her. I teased open her folds and slid my tongue up and down. "What's wrong?"

"Stop. Please. It's too much."

She was shoving me away from her so I paused, lifting my mouth from her tender moisture. "Stop?" I glanced up at her, nostrils flaring. "Is that what you want me to do?"

Miranda was biting her bottom lip. Her cheeks were flushed pink, a stain blooming above her breasts, which were still bursting above her neckline. Even as she stood there making up her mind, her hips rocked toward me, offering herself. But I waited, despite the fact that it made me want to pull my dick out and shove it inside that hot offering. "Tell me what to do, baby," I urged her. My breath caused goose bumps to rise on her inner thighs.

"Don't stop," she said.

Triumph burst over me. I had her. It was the best fucking feeling imaginable. "No? What should I do?" I flicked my tongue over her. "This? Is this what you want?"

She gave a soft moan. "Yes, that's what I want. More. Please."

"So polite. You don't have to be polite with me. Tell me what you want. Make me do it."

"Ple—"

She stopped herself. "Do it. Go down on me. Lick me."

Her chest was rising up and down rapidly. Her eyes were glassy, her embarrassment warring with her desire.

I couldn't ask for more. She had just given me the most she could give and I respected that. I loved it. "I would fucking love to," I told her. Then I hauled her left leg up off the floor and hooked it over my shoulder so I could access her as deeply and thoroughly as I craved.

She gasped at the move but didn't protest and when I lowered my mouth to her again, sucking on her clit briefly before plunging into the depths of her heat, it only took her a few seconds to shatter. She came apart, screaming out my name in a way that had me pulling back frantically after she settled back down. I was going to have her and it was a moment I didn't want to lose.

So I undid my pants and instinctively went for a condom. Then I realized I didn't have to. I knew I was clean and I trusted Miranda was. For the first time in my entire life I could enter a woman without anything between us and what better person for that than Miranda.

Her leg had slid back to the floor when I rose, but I hauled it back up around my hip, grateful that she was a dancer. Still in heels, it wasn't a struggle for her. Briefly, I pulled back so I could drink in the sight of her, disheveled and glowing with the orgasm I gave her, firm thighs wrapped around me.

"You're the most beautiful woman I've ever seen," I told her and I meant it.

Then I directed my cock and pushed straight inside her.

It was like fucking coming home.

I HAD NO ability to think, to speak, or to stop Alejandro. I didn't want to. He had me wide open while I was still recovering from the intensity of my orgasm. It had been intimate and wet and amazing and now here he was—suddenly inside me. Big and demanding and perfect.

For the first time I saw his control slip. His eyes closed briefly and he swore under his breath. My feelings exactly. I was clinging to his arms, needing support, my legs shaking. My entire body felt liquid. Hot, dripping liquid.

"Miranda," he growled.

I had never heard my name spoken like that. It was almost overwhelming, the intensity of what was happening between us. It was raw sex, spiraling without thought to consequence. Yet I had never wanted anything as much in my life. "Fuck me," I said, a breathy, demanding whisper. "Now."

His eyes darkened. Resting his hand on the wall, he gave me what I wanted. Slick, hard thrusts, the room quiet except for the sound of skin on skin, and our frantic breathing. It felt like it went on and on, our bodies in tune, the tightening in my core growing and growing until I felt like I would burst. But I wanted to stay there, forever, in this moment, my nails digging into his hard muscles, clawing at his skin. My head was slamming into the wall but I welcomed the beat of it, the distraction that kept me from going totally under and drowning.

"Don't hold back," he demanded. "Come for me."

I squeezed my eyes shut. I couldn't look at him. It was too much. All too much. He was shredding my emotions, stripping me down. He was stretching my inner walls, filling me with his huge cock, his invasive presence. I had gotten more than I knew how to handle and I held tightly against it, afraid.

"Don't you dare fucking hide from me," he said.

A light slap landed on the side of my ass where he was holding my leg up, startling me into opening my eyes. "What was that for?" I asked, though I knew. And I liked it.

His hand shifted further behind me until he was squeezing my ass, forcing a deeper collision between us. "That was for you holding out on me. I want it all."

Then he kissed me and it was so hot and so much and he was so everywhere all over me that I couldn't keep my wall in place anymore. It tumbled to the ground and I came with a fierce desperate cry that had him exclaiming in triumph. His thrusts were furious as my body clenched on to him, thoughts scattered to the wind.

"Baby," he said. "You're so damn hot."

When it all was done crashing, when our squeezing and

gripping and crying out eased, we stood there, staring at each other, panting. I was shell-shocked. It was like Alejandro had tossed a land mine onto my life and I was staring at him through the rubble and settling dust. He had exploded my carefully planned future with his mouth, his fingers, his big thick cock.

Neither of us spoke. Words were too trite. I wanted a minute to pick up the shattered pieces of my soul. This hadn't been just sex. This had been... something.

And it scared the living shit out of me.

Then he made it worse by drawing his thumb across my bottom lip, his dark eyes bright with emotion. First he lingered there, then he withdrew his finger and touched his lips to the corner of my mouth, followed by the other. Then he rested his forehead against mine, encapsulating me, absorbing my space, my air. It felt like it hung on and on and with each heartbeat he took more from me until I felt like I was disappearing, smothered by his body, his presence.

"I can't breathe," I murmured, pressing against the wall, my hands flying up to stave off his chest. It was too much.

"Sorry," he said, instantly pulling back at the pressure of my push. He eased my leg off his hip until my foot settled on the floor. "Are you okay?" he asked. With his free hand he lifted my top back over my bare breasts.

I was still damp and throbbing and my legs were shaky but I nodded. I wasn't sure I was okay, exactly, but I wasn't hurt either, and I couldn't articulate my feelings. I could just nod.

When he shifted, disengaging himself from my body, I was further confused because I felt the loss profoundly. When he was too close, I didn't want it, then when he pulled back, I didn't want that either. My cheeks flushed as I grew angry with myself. I was an adult. I had agreed to this. Hell, I had asked for it. Literally.

Time to pull it together. I was a strong woman. It was up to me to break this weird aura, to make it normal again. Casual. "It's a good thing I'm in shape," I said. "Or you might have crippled me."

For a brief moment I thought he was disappointed in my words, but then he flashed me a grin. "You can always lean on me more. I've got you."

That's what I was afraid of. That he would want this again and so would I. "Thanks." I shimmied my pants back up in place, peeling myself off the wall. "I'll be right back." I needed to go to the bathroom because there had been zero condom used here and I could feel the result of that making its way sluggishly down my thigh.

The timing was off, but stranger things had happened. The thought that we had just conceived a child made heat crawl up my neck and settle in my cheeks and my mouth to go dry. I was ready to be a mother, but this? All of this emotion and messiness wasn't what I had pictured.

His eyes lingered on me and his hand slid down my arm. I half expected him to stop me or follow me but he did neither. In the bathroom I took care of business then stared at myself in the mirror. I looked feverish and well fucked. Splashing water on my face, I patted my cheeks dry with my shirt. I hadn't unpacked the towels yet. Then I ditched my heels and went back in to the living room, weaving around boxes. Alejandro was where I had left him, in the entryway. But he was zipped back up, shirt on. His phone was in his hand.

I realized he was intending to leave.

Anger and disappointment and mortification all welled up in me. "You heading out?" I asked, impressed with how light and casual I sounded.

"I'm going to get some fried chicken."

That made me blink. "What?"

"I'm starving. Sex makes me hungry. You want anything? I'll be back in ten minutes."

"No. I'm fine." Then I thought about it. I didn't have to watch my weight as carefully now that I wasn't on tour. I could indulge just a little. "Sure. I'll take whatever they have. I like thighs."

"I'm a breast man myself."

That made me laugh, despite my discomfort. "You're a cheesy man, that's what you are."

"Come here."

I wanted to protest. To tell him that if he wanted something he could come to me. But I found I wanted his touch, his comfort, more than I wanted to be defiant. "What?" I asked as I walked up to him. I felt tiny in front of him without the armor of my heels.

A wave of tenderness washed through me. I saw glimpses of the sweet boy I had known merged with the aggressive and sensual adult man. I tickled his beard with the tips of my fingers. "You need to shave."

"You didn't mind a few minutes ago." He shifted out of my touch.

So he liked to tease but not be teased in return. Interesting. I smiled, enjoying some semblance of power. "Go get your chicken."

He bent down and kissed me. It felt strange and inevitable all at the same time. "I'll be right back."

"I like honey mustard sauce."

"Yes, ma'am." He sauntered to the front door and left, a sexually satisfied man.

I breathed a sigh of relief. I was glad he was coming back but at the same time I was glad to have a minute to myself. I needed to find the stupid bath towels and take a shower and find my equilibrium again.

After he exited the house, I stood there in the doorway and watched him head down the walk. It was dark outside now, and after a moment of staring at his back, I shook off my reverie and went back into the house. My house. All nine hundred adorable retro square feet of it. Tomorrow I was going to go out and buy a pink lawn flamingo. The house was screaming for it.

But all of that seemed dimmed now by the enormity of what Alejandro and I had just done. My thighs rubbed together, sticky and warm, and I had both a seed of hope and a tremor of fear that we might have made a baby.

I took a deep breath and started for the shower when there was a knock on my door. Thinking it was Alejandro I opened it without thought. "Hi, did you forget something? Chicken doesn't fry that fast." The smile fell off my face when I realized it wasn't him.

It was a man in his late thirties to forties, dark hair, a dark beard. He was holding a cat. But not like an animal lover. His hand was twisted in the cat's scruff and he had him dangled in front of his body far enough to cause me instant alarm.

"Is this your fucking cat?" he asked.

The little guy was orange and looked healthy, not like a stray. "No," I said. "It's not. Why?" I wanted to reach out and snatch the cat away from the guy. Then I realized there was no reason why I couldn't if the cat wasn't his. So I wrapped my hands around his furry middle and told the guy, "I've got him, you can let go."

"Good." He wiped his hand on his shirt like he was offended by the feel of the fur. "This asshole cat gets in my trash all the time and makes a fucking mess."

"I'm sorry to hear that. You can just leave him with me and I'll find the owner and let them know."

He gave a nod. Then he glanced behind me. "Did you just move in?"

His interest made me uncomfortable. My gut instinct was telling me this was not a guy who was totally right in the head. I wondered if I smelled like sex. Or if anyone had heard the wall banging, our mutual cries of pleasure. Heat bloomed in my cheeks and I nodded, easily letting a lie fall off my lips. "Yes, my boyfriend and I."

Briefly he locked eyes with me and I fought the urge to shiver. Listen to your gut, everyone always says. Well mine was saying this guy was trouble. A pervert. Dangerous. I gave him a bland smile, holding the cat closer to my chest.

"I live next door. I'm Conrad."

"Lola." I didn't really want to give my name but I didn't want to piss this guy off. So I just tossed out another lie, plucking the first name that popped into my head. It rolled off the tongue before I could consider the implications of being dishonest with the person who shared a wall with me. But years of touring had given me a sense of who was just annoying and who was actually creepy. This guy was off, which sucked. This rental was where I wanted to have a baby.

Maybe he would move.

Maybe he had a wife who was nice and I was just paranoid.

He just nodded and turned to leave. I shut the door as quickly as I could without arousing suspicion and locked it. I buried my head into the cat's neck. He smelled clean. Not like he had been digging through the trash. That was a red flag. Interesting. I dug around and checked for a tag.

There was a collar and a little silver tag.

Max.

I started, my throat tightening. "Hey, buddy," I said to him. "Now that's a weird coincidence, huh?"

The orange cat meowed loudly, nudging his head into my hand. He was purring.

"The man next door is a prick, huh?" I murmured. "Let's call your owner."

When I called the number on the tag, it started ringing. Then I heard an actual phone ringing, faintly, on the other side of the shared wall with my grumpy neighbor. That struck me as yet another odd coincidence. I quickly ended the call. The phone next door went silent. I called a second time and there it was again. A ringing.

I ended the second call and stood there, heart pounding quickly. "What is going on?" I asked Max. If his name really was Max. Why would the guy next door claim it wasn't his cat but the phone was ringing in his apartment? Was he trying to rid himself of his girlfriend's cat? Did he have a sick sense of humor? Was he trying to case my apartment, check me out?

There was no explanation that was anything short of fucked up.

So carrying the cat into the kitchen, I got him a bowl of water, and myself a weapon. I had a .22 packed away in the boxes in my bedroom but for now a knife would do. I knew how to use it. Max had taught me, just in case I ever needed to get out of a tough situation.

I had only had to use that skill once.

Fortunately, I was awesome at labeling boxes and it only took two minutes to find the one with the knives. As soon as I had it in my hand, I called Alejandro. He was a bodyguard after all.

Aware of how thin the walls clearly were I went into the

bathroom, closed the door, turned on the faucet.

"Hey, what's up?" he asked. "Do you want to add biscuits to your order? I just walked in the restaurant."

"Yeah, that would be great." My stomach rumbled. Apparently sex made me hungry too. "But I'm calling because my neighbor stopped by with a cat."

"What?"

I explained what had just happened. "Don't you think that's weird?"

"Was he hitting on you? Because I would hit on you if you moved in next door."

That made me roll my eyes even though no one could see me. "No. His manner was not flirtatious. It was more like he wanted to skin me alive and wear me like a woman suit."

"Wow. Okay. I didn't expect you to say that. Are you scared? Should I skip the chicken and come back now?"

I hesitated. I was a little freaked out but ten minutes wouldn't matter. "No, it's fine, you can get the chicken. I told him you were my boyfriend." Saying it out loud to Alejandro embarrassed me. It sounded… presumptuous. Like I wanted that now that we had had sex.

He cleared his throat. "Smart thinking." His tone was neutral, not possessive the way it had been earlier.

I felt oddly deflated. He sounded like he had in Lola's hotel. Friendly and familiar, but nothing more. Not like he had buried his cock in me ten minutes earlier and destroyed everything I thought

I knew about him. About us.

It seemed like he was asking a silent question. *What do you want from me?*

Or maybe that was just me projecting. What did I want? I had no idea. But I did know I wanted him to make sure my neighbor didn't hassle me. "So maybe you come back over in the next day or two and help me sort out who this cat actually belongs to?" I immediately realized that sounded like I was just angling to spend more time with Alejandro. It sounded lame.

I quickly added, "And give Conrad next door a friendly hint that you carry a gun?" Conrad didn't need to know I was carrying. He might just see that as a sexy challenge.

Men were fucked up.

Men also thought women were weak and I knew my greatest weapon was catching any assailant off guard. No one expected me to be able to defend myself.

"I can do that. I would be really good at making sure this guy knows you have someone looking out for you." His voice lowered. "I'm spending the night tonight. That was already my plan, you know."

My body instantly responded to his tone and I was annoyed with myself for the tightness in my core, the instant ache I felt. "You really should wait for an invitation."

He gave a low laugh. "My invitation was you coming for me twice."

My nipples tightened instantly. "Aren't you in a chicken joint? Can't people hear you?"

"I don't care. And I'm staying over tonight. I won't be able to sleep if I think you're in danger."

"I don't think I'm in danger, exactly, but I would like to send the right message right off the bat." That I may look pretty but I was no sitting duck, and I had some muscle to back me up.

"Does that mean you'll make out with me on the front step?"

That shouldn't sound as appealing to me as it did. To want to declare publicly that we were something more than old friends. "That's negotiable."

"I don't negotiate." Alejandro sounded cocksure of himself. "Hold on." He shifted the phone and I could hear him ordering food.

I hung up. It's a personal pet peeve to be put on hold on the phone and he had pushed all my buttons, intentionally. While I still hadn't been able to jump in the shower and wash him off of me yet.

He called right back. "Did you do that on purpose?"

"Yes. You don't negotiate? I don't get put on hold."

Alejandro gave a low whistle. "Damn. Then I guess I better get back to you immediately if not sooner. And give you whatever you want."

That I would be willing to wait for. Except I had no idea what I wanted.

All I knew for certain was that I was eager for Alejandro to get back.

And put his tongue all over me again.

CHAPTER 7

returned to the house with my food, having bitten half of Miranda's biscuit en route, not really particularly concerned about the dude living next door. He was probably just hot for Miranda and wanted an excuse to talk to her. I could hardly blame the guy for that. I'd been hot for her for a decade.

Now I'd had her. It had been better than I could have ever pictured, and I had pictured it frequently. She was so sweet and compliant, but so damn sexy. She was the perfect woman and now that I'd had her I was feeling greedy. I wanted more.

But it wasn't just the physical. Something had shifted between us, beyond the pleasure of sex. Sex can be fun, satisfying, relaxing, rough. This had been… intimate. Bonding. Like I had breathed her inside of me. Like I had imprinted on her.

That thought had me shaking my head as I went up the walk. What, was I a fucking poet all of a sudden?

I hadn't just gone for chicken. I had gone to collect my thoughts so I could be normal around her. It was a good move. I felt in control again, even if I had a video playing on repeat in my head of me thrusting into her warm heat without a condom, the way her eyes had rolled back, and she had bit her lip in ecstatic anguish.

Miranda answered her door with a knife in her hand. That was unexpected. I eyed it. "What the hell are you planning to do with that?"

"Kill someone if necessary."

"Damn." I shook my head as I stepped into her duplex. "Remind me not to piss you off." She was holding the weapon correctly. Firm grip. Ready to gut.

"Too late," she said. "You already have today. But I forgive you because you helped me move and you're pretending to be my boyfriend."

Part of me wanted to ask what specifically I had done, other than get a little bossy and demanding, but I didn't want her to get indignant all over again. The house was a jumble of boxes and furniture haphazardly placed and I realized after I ate I was going to have to do something about the mess for her. This was too much for her to tackle at nine at night. "If you're telling your neighbor I live here, I wouldn't be knocking on your front door."

"That is a good point." She bent over, and my throat tightened.

Damn, she had a hot body. I wanted that, all of that. Tonight and every night after that. There was the rub. I had thought all I wanted was a taste of her, but she was everything I had expected and more and now I couldn't quit the idea of us repeating earlier. Daily. I wondered if she had showered while I was gone or if she still wore me on her. My scent. My cum.

My cock started to swell again, thinking about how close her head was to it. If she just shifted and opened her mouth...

"Look at this little guy," she said, standing back up with a large cat in her arms. He was all fluff and fat and lazy attitude. He didn't even attempt to help her hold him but lay there as dead weight, fully trusting her. He was clearly a house cat, not a stray or an outdoor cat belonging to one of the houses nearby.

"That's definitely an indoor cat. He's in serious need of a gym membership." His stomach rolls were spilling over Miranda's arm.

Miranda laughed. "Hush. He's just big-boned."

"Yeah, that's what my aunt Freda says too and it's a lie. It's called empanadas at midnight."

"This cat is not eating empanadas at midnight." She squeezed him tighter. "And don't be mean. You'll give him body image issues."

That made me snort. "All right, are you calling the number on this collar or am I?"

"Why don't you call it?"

"Sure." I flicked the tag over and pulled out my phone.

Miranda was right. I could instantly hear it ringing in the attached apartment next door. That was weird. "Can you put the knife down?" I murmured to her. "You're making me nervous."

I had never seen Miranda wielding a weapon and with a cat

in her arms. It was a strange juxtaposition I couldn't like. Miranda and violence didn't go hand in hand and frankly I was afraid she would accidentally nick herself and the chubby cat.

"Hello?" It was a man's voice. Gruff and scratchy.

"Yeah, hi, I found your cat. The orange guy."

Miranda was mouthing a name to me but I couldn't understand what she was saying. I just shook my head.

"I don't have a cat."

Interesting. "Your number is on his tag."

"Well, I don't know why because I don't have a cat."

"Okay then. Sorry to bother you." I ended the call and frowned. "He's denying the cat is his."

"I'm telling you, the guy next door is nuts." Miranda bit her lip. She kissed the top of the cat's head and set him down. "I'm so upset. I love this house. I don't want a creeper next door. Why would he say the cat isn't his?"

"The cat looks well cared for, too. This is strange." I couldn't figure out the strategy or end plan if this was some kind of setup. "What is his name, by the way?"

"Max." Her cheeks flushed.

I froze. "Max? Are you for real?"

She nodded. "Can you believe that? Crazy coincidence, huh?"

Except I don't believe in coincidences. "I'm going over there."

I tried to hear the guy's voice in my head again. But I hadn't been paying close attention. But obviously if it was Max, Miranda would have known.

"What are you going to say?"

"Don't worry about it, I'm charming." I was going to tell him to fuck off, but in a friendly way. "I won't kill him unless I have to." Her face grew alarmed. "I'm joking." Sort of.

"I'm going with you."

"Just stay here."

"No."

Given the mulish look on her face, I decided it wasn't worth it to argue. "Fine."

We walked the three feet to the neighbor's house and I knocked, noting again the flowers in pots, the chairs for porch sitting. It didn't indicate a crazy loner lived there. We waited. No one answered. I knocked again.

Miranda frowned at me. "We heard him inside," she whispered.

I shrugged and gave a third knock. Nothing. I couldn't hear a TV or anything. So I decided to go around the back of the house and poke around a little.

"Where are you going?" she asked in a fierce whisper. "You can't go back there."

"Why not?" I asked mildly. "Isn't it your yard too?"

"We have separate patios."

"Then I'm just getting the lay of the land." I winked at her. "It's my yard too since we're so hot and heavy."

"I don't think this is a good idea. I left the knife in the house."

That made me snort. "I don't need a knife and neither do you. Promise me you won't get into a habit of strolling around the yard all jumpy with a freaking knife in your hand." That was a downright terrifying image.

"I can take care of myself," she said.

I wasn't going to argue that point with her, but I hoped the neighbor was just a regular Joe and we were being overly cautious.

The house had a fair amount of scrubby foliage, like most yards in Miami that weren't tended to on a regular basis. It was overgrown but half of it was dead. The back stucco hadn't been repaired in years and the windows looked original. I knew Miranda had been attracted to the nostalgic feel but the place was kind of a dump. Each patio was enclosed by a low-slung cinder block wall. Very midcentury.

I went right up to the window of the apartment next door and looked inside, expecting to see him in his kitchen. Nothing.

"You're being too obvious," Miranda said. Her stage whisper sounded fretful.

I just waved her off. Being obvious was talking so that someone would hear us.

The kitchen and the room beyond it had almost no furniture in it. Something felt off. It looked more like a surveillance setup than an actual apartment. There was no fridge in the kitchen and the countertop was littered with electronics, not a toaster or a coffeemaker. There was a laptop and a scanner and a small table with two chairs. Not okay. Every alarm inside me went off.

Was it a drug dealer's house? That seemed unlikely. This looked like an FBI setup. Who were they watching though? There would be no reason to follow Miranda. Maybe it was the prior residents in her side of the duplex.

Or maybe, worst of all, it was somehow related to Max.

I nudged Miranda and nodded my head in the direction of her side of the duplex. She understood and walked quickly to her patio. "The back door to my side is locked."

"Just keep going around to the front."

She obeyed and within a minute we were back in her apartment. "I'm not letting you live here alone," I told her. "I'm moving in until we figure out what the fuck is going on."

Her jaw dropped. "What? What did you see in the kitchen?"

Nothing good. "No one is living there. The living room is basically empty and the kitchen has no small appliances or a refrigerator. It looks more like an interview room."

"Maybe it's just not rented? Or maybe that guy is renting it but lives somewhere else?"

"Why would anyone do that? It doesn't look like a drug house or a flop pad." I wasn't quite sure what I was looking at but I knew I didn't like it. That wasn't normal. Especially given that the guy had come over with the cat. The cat he denied owning who was named Max and whose collar had a number that rang to a phone on the other side of that wall. Nope. Didn't like this shit at all.

Miranda looked as concerned as I felt. "I don't know but I feel like I need to turn on a floor fan or something to create white noise. Doesn't it feel like we're being listened to?"

Her voice was low and she had moved to the wall farthest from the shared wall.

"The guy isn't home. If he was he would have to have super human hearing." Unless the apartment was bugged. I would have to do a sweep. I dialed a number on my phone. "But I have an idea."

Wester, a co-worker at Miami Security, answered my call. "What's up?"

"Hey, listen, can you run something for me? I want to know who owns a building and who is living there now."

"Why can't you do that yourself?"

"Because I'm busy."

"And I'm just sitting around doing nothing?"

"Probably. You answered your phone, didn't you?" Wester was probably with his girlfriend, Olivia, and now that I thought about it, she lived only a few minutes from Miranda's apartment. "You at Olivia's?"

"Yeah, why?"

"Can you come over to 25th Street? I'm at my friend Miranda's and I want your opinion on the situation next door."

There was rustling and Wester cleared his throat. "Is it serious or can it wait, man?"

"It's life or death." It wasn't even close to that but if I had an opportunity to cock block a friend, I was taking it. I ruined it by allowing too much glee to slip into my voice.

"You're an asshole," he said. "But fine, I'll come over now, then I'm turning my fucking phone off for the rest of the night."

"Perfect, thanks. I owe you one." I ended the call and shot

Wester a text with the address. "Another bodyguard is coming over to give his opinion on the situation. I want to make sure this place isn't wired."

"Okay." Miranda was unpacking a box of books.

"What are you doing?" I asked, even though it was obvious.

She stacked them onto a bookcase, working quickly. "I'm freaked out. I have to keep busy. This day has not gone according to plan."

Obviously I could understand her being a little afraid. The situation was weird. But did she mean sex with me as well? I sat on the couch and watched her, finally getting the chance to eat my chicken. Miranda's hair had slipped loose of the messy bun she had put it in and was drooping down her back. I wanted to go up behind her and shift her hair aside and kiss her neck.

I wanted to slide my cock inside her again, from behind this time. But she was too distracted now.

What the fuck was going on here? Was it no big deal or was it something shady? I had a nagging feeling, one I could precisely place. It was the ominous sense of helplessness I had always felt when Max pulled his latest bullshit. This smelled like Max. I had never considered the possibility that Max would have kept tabs on Miranda over the years but it made total sense.

Max was a control freak. He wouldn't want her to move on.

He would also enjoy fucking with her, or at least any men who might be in her life.

And sick as it was, I couldn't help but feel smug. If he was watching her, then he knew she wanted my baby. Then he would know that we had sex, and that she had enjoyed every second of it.

But I didn't see how Max's reach would extend to Miami if he were somewhere else entirely.

I hoped Mickey would get some information for me soon.

And I actually hoped Max was in town. Because I wanted him to understand that I wasn't a teenager anymore. I wasn't tolerating his manipulative sociopath bullshit this time. I would outsmart the narcissistic prick and expose him to the world as a liar, a thief, and a cold-hearted bastard. Especially to Miranda. I didn't want to hurt her. But I wanted her to be able to move on from Max and clearly that wasn't going to happen until she saw him for what he was.

That thought had me standing up and acting on my earlier impulse. I set my fried chicken back on the table and I came up behind Miranda and touched her hair at the nape of her neck. She jumped.

"Jeez, you move like a ninja!" She tried to turn around to face me but I took both of her hands in mine and then placed them palm down on the top of the waist-high bookcase. "What are you doing?" she asked, sounding breathless and instantly aroused.

"Helping you relax." I shifted so that I was very close to her, the front of my shorts brushing against her tight ass. I had an instant hard-on. She was just so ripe and firm and juicy and I wanted more. Her shirt was off the shoulder and still holding her hands so she couldn't push me off, I ran my lips softly over her exposed flesh. "Your skin is so soft."

"Alejandro," she said, drawing out all the syllables of my name.

Most people fired off my name, quick, staccato. When I was a child and my mother was angry, she got louder, higher-pitched, faster. Even in my flirtations my name felt more accusation than endearment, yet as it rolled out over the plump sexy lips of Miranda it sounded intimate, slow. I hoped like hell the guy next door would check out as not suspicious at all.

I wanted to get back to us. Me and Miranda, fully naked and in her bed. So I could taste her slowly, head to toe, satisfy my every desire, fantasy I had ever had about her, before I sank into her moist heat and brought her to orgasm while I stared into her beautiful brown eyes.

"Yes?" I asked, lifting my lips briefly before I went back to kissing her, worshipping her flesh, sucking softly on the vein in her neck.

"This isn't good timing. Isn't your friend coming over?"

"It will take him ten minutes."

I paused, giving her time to voice a legitimate protest, but she was silent. The only sound in the room was her breathing and the hum of the air conditioning.

Threading my fingers through hers, I pressed my cock against her, wanting to push her a little, wanting a response. I felt high, intense, the memory of how tight she had been around my cock driving me to be reckless. Her body arched toward me, ass knocking against me. She was going to let me fuck her again and it was going to be amazing.

There was a knock on the door.

Miranda jumped.

Disappointed, I stepped back, releasing her. I supposed I deserved that after dragging Wester out here. He was cock blocking right back.

"I'll get it."

Miranda cleared her throat. "We're going to continue this conversation later."

"Were we talking?"

She looked both aroused and troubled. "Maybe we're not talking enough."

I wanted her gut reaction, not whatever logic she might settle on. I ignored her concern. "Have a biscuit. You must be starving. I haven't seen you eat all day."

Glancing out the living room window by lifting one of the slats of the blinds, I saw Wester with his girlfriend. I pulled the door open. "Hey, man, thanks for coming." I held my hand out to do a shake and a shoulder bump. "Olivia, nice to see you again."

Wester's girlfriend was blond and beautiful and damn smart. She was a grad student and generally speaking makeup-free and wearing jeans or shorts and a T-shirt. That's what she was wearing now, along with a smile. "Hi, Alejandro. What's going on?"

"Come on in. Sorry to interrupt your night. Though I probably saved you from terrible sex with your boyfriend."

She laughed. "Gee, thanks. So kind of you."

"This is Miranda Bartello, who just moved into this place.

Miranda, Wester and Olivia."

Miranda was eyeing Olivia. "I've met you before! Aren't you Ricardo's wife? I was at a party at your house last year."

"Oh, that's actually my identical twin sister, Eva. Yeah, she lives the high life. What were you doing at a party there, are you friends with Ricardo?"

I wanted to know the answer to that as well. Ricardo was filthy rich but also shady as fuck. He had a side business dealing drugs, but mostly his money was made in pharmaceutical monopolies.

But Miranda just shook her head. "I don't know Ricardo really. This was at an event for celebrities during the EMT festival and I was there with Lola Brandy. I've been a backup dancer and body double for her for two years."

"Oh wow, that's cool."

It was cool. I wondered if Miranda knew how cool she really was. She tended to downplay herself a little, surrounded as she had been for years by huge egos. She wasn't one to brag about herself, but I thought she was really damn accomplished. "She beat out like two hundred people for that job," I said.

"Alejandro, I don't think they care about that," she said, looking embarrassed.

"I care. You should be proud of what you've done."

She laughed. "Thanks, Dad."

"Just curious," Olivia said. "What did you think of Ricardo? Because I can't stand my brother-in-law."

Wester gave her a look. "You can't ask someone a loaded

question like that. Totally awkward, Liv."

"Sorry, that's a fair point. I just really hate him so let's just strike that question from the record."

"No, it's fine. I barely met him. But I can't say I had a particularly fabulous response to Ricardo. He told me I was cute enough but I could benefit from a nose job."

"That's Ricardo." Olivia shook her head.

"You don't need a nose job," I said, annoyed. Miranda was beautiful just the way she was.

"I'm okay with my nose. That wasn't my point. It's all good." Then Miranda waved her hands around. "I'm so sorry for the mess. Today was moving day, and I am a little behind in my unpacking, but I did find the glasses and I went to the store. Can I get you anything to drink?"

How ridiculous was that? She was playing hostess. Actually, it was the cutest damn thing ever. What was ridiculous was how damn proud of her I was. I looked at her and saw an amazing person. Humble, kind, put-together. Adept at making people feel comfortable. I wanted her to be mine. I wanted this to be my house and her my wife, with our child sleeping in the other room.

The need hit me hard, catching me off guard. Sure, I had always crushed on Miranda. I had been fixated on having sex with her, fulfilling that fantasy, and it had been better than I had ever expected. But fuck, this was more than that and it scared the shit out of me. I needed to get a fucking grip and take a step back. This was about Miranda. What she wanted. Her fresh start. Her new life. It wasn't about me.

I didn't know how I felt about being a father. But I did know how I felt about Miranda being a mother. She would be amazing.

And I wanted to knock her up. I wanted to give her a baby, whether I was involved with the child or not.

Both Wester and Olivia said no, thanks to Miranda's offer of a drink so I explained to Wester about the appearance of the cat, who was currently rubbing against Olivia's leg, raising his head for her to rub. She complied and said, "Hi, cutie."

I gestured to the apartment next door. "Wes, you've got to see this." Before Miranda could speak I said, "Stay here this time." Then because it sounded so dominant, I added a token, "Please."

I expected her to protest but she stayed silent.

This time I cut through the back yard and showed Wester the eerie emptiness of the apartment next door. It didn't take him long to come to the same conclusion as me. "That's surveillance. Dude, I would sweep Miranda's apartment for bugs and cameras. Maybe the guy is just a pervert. Maybe it's something else. Does she have anything in her past, a stalker?"

"Not that I'm aware of but I'll ask her more questions." If I were honest with myself, I didn't know dick about Miranda's life. Not even when she had been with Max, but definitely not in the years since. "But I know I can't let her stay here alone until I've gone through it."

Wester shook his head. "Fuck no. I'll help you check the apartment."

"Thanks. I had known this was totally off but I was glad that somehow my emotions weren't just clouding the situation, you know what I'm saying?"

His eyebrows shot up. "So why exactly are you emotional about Miranda? Is this a new thing because I thought you were all about the hit and quit."

"Miranda was dating my brother when I was in high school. I just care about her that's all."

Now Wester looked more than a little surprised. "You have a brother? I had no idea."

"Yes."

"Where does he live?"

We had retraced our steps and we were on Miranda's patio. I didn't want her to hear me talking about Max negatively. I had already made my position pretty damn clear. I didn't want her to think I was harping on it. But I couldn't lie either. "No fucking clue," I said. "Miranda thinks he's dead but I think he just bounced. Just rolled out and left her."

"Damn." Wester rubbed his chin. "Were they still together at the time?"

I nodded. "She thinks he was abducted. Mistaken identity in a drug deal gone wrong. I think he was walking away from a crime he didn't want to get busted for."

Wester eyed me. "Do you know for a fact that he was involved in illegal activity?"

"I'm ninety-nine percent sure. He mentioned things." Usually bragging because he always thought he was smarter than everyone else.

"Do you really think she didn't know anything then? I mean, most people know if someone they're having sex with has secrets."

The reminder that Miranda had been Max's first made my blood boil. I didn't want to think about her having sex with him. Her body was mine now. The jealousy made me want to reach for her, but I held back the urge.

I had always assumed that Miranda was kept in the dark by Max. He never straight out told me anything. So why would he tell her, who was on the straight and narrow? It didn't seem like something she would just be cool with. "I don't know. She doesn't seem the type to stay with him if she knew what he was doing." But it made me think.

What did I really know about the past?

It made me want the information from Mickey even more. It also made me want to pick through all of Max's old shit. All of that was at my parents' house. I would head over there tomorrow after work.

"What was he doing at the time he went missing?"

"Like the specific day? I have no idea. I never asked." I didn't.

When Miranda had called my parents frantic after a day or two of no contact with Max all I had felt was relief. Total relief.

But that wasn't what I felt now.

Now I was eager. If Max was around, I could finally slam my fist into his face and tell the motherfucking weasel what exactly I thought of him.

"Maybe you should ask Miranda what she knows."

"Maybe I will." Did I really want to go there though? Did I want the truth even if it was an ugly one?

I yanked open the back door and came face-to-face with Miranda pointing a gun at me.

CHAPTER 8

"Do you hear that?" I asked Olivia as we chatted in the kitchen. "I hear something next door." Carefully I moved across the linoleum floor and put my ear to the wall.

"What? No, I don't hear anything." Olivia moved closer to me.

"It's someone walking." I moved back. "Someone has been in there this whole time. I need to tell Alejandro." But first I was going for my gun. "Wait here. I've got to grab something."

"Okay." Olivia sounded bewildered. I wondered if she thought I was totally nuts because she seemed like someone I could actually be friends with. I needed some new friends in town. Nor did I want people to think I was a crazy woman.

But I couldn't worry about that right now. Something was totally off next door. I wanted to know what it was because damn it, I had rented this duplex for twelve months. I did not want someone destroying my peace of mind. But I also knew that

112

tonight I wouldn't be able to sleep there. Aside from the fact that I was freaked out, the bed wasn't even in place and I had no clue where the box with my sheets was. The latter part of the move had not gone according to plan thanks to Conrad the cat guy.

Before that, Alejandro had been more than a distraction. He had shattered my world. My body and my mind.

Feeling anxious, I texted Lola while I was looking through the boxes in my bedroom for the one I needed. She texted me back right away giving me the response I wanted. She was a generous and kind person who didn't mind sharing her success and I had been counting on that.

Spying the box I wanted I tore off the tape and dug through it for my lock box. The key was on my key ring so I took the whole box into the kitchen and opened it. I wasn't going to bother to load the gun. I just wanted to scare Conrad if he appeared to be threatening Alejandro.

The back door to my kitchen went flying open and without hesitation I spun and pointed the gun straight at the intruder.

It was just Alejandro eyeing me.

"That better not be loaded," Alejandro said. "Because I don't feel like taking a bullet today."

I lowered my arm. "Why would I shoot you? I thought you were Conrad or whatever the hell his name is."

He was still just eyeing me like he'd thought I had lost my mind. "Why do you have a gun?"

"I'm a single lady. I need to protect myself."

"Do you have a license? Have you had training?"

"Yes, of course." The gun felt natural in my hand at my side. I had plenty of training at the range. It wasn't like I walked around shooting it randomly.

I had only fired it once outside of the range.

The day before Max left.

"Can you believe this?" Alejandro asked Wester. "She's hot and carrying. Should I be worried?"

"You should be terrified." Wester grinned. "Hey, I'm all for it. You heard her. She's a single lady. She should be able to protect herself."

"How would you feel if I got a gun?" Olivia asked him.

He frowned. "Why would you need a gun? You're a grad student in a low-risk lifestyle."

Olivia looked at me, amused. "Do you hear how sexy my boyfriend makes me sound? I have a low-risk lifestyle."

I had questions of curiosity about how they had met. I hadn't liked her brother-in-law, Ricardo, the one and only time I had been to his house. He was a flirt and an arrogant one at that. He was the classic rich guy who thought because he had money he could get whatever he wanted at all times—including women. But there wasn't really time to have a friendly conversation because I was convinced the creeper next door was sitting in a dark and empty apartment, listening to us. I wasn't usually paranoid but this guy had me with permanent goose bumps up my spine.

"I thought I had a low-risk lifestyle," I told her.

"That's crap. You're a body double," Alejandro commented. "And why did you pull a gun again? Let's get back to that."

"Yes, let's get back to that." I gestured to the apartment next door. "Someone is over there. I heard footsteps."

His eyebrows rose. "Then let's go over there."

I shook my head. "He's not going to answer the door obviously. And I am no advocate of breaking and entering."

Alejandro looked at me like I was insane. "Me either. I'm not looking for charges against me."

I set the gun on the kitchen counter. "Okay, so what I'm going to do is leave here tonight and stay at Lola's house. Then tomorrow I will have cameras installed outside and better locks put on the door."

He nodded. "I'm going to figure out who rented the other half of this house. Where does Lola live? I can drive you there."

He gave me a look, one that said he would not be dropping me off. He planned to stay with me and damn it, I wanted him to. My cheeks felt warm.

"Her house is in North Beach, off Alton." I looked around and sighed. "This was not how I pictured this day ending. What a disappointment."

"It hasn't all been disappointing."

Oh good Lord, did he have to be so obvious? His voice was filled with innuendo. "No, I suppose not," I said wryly.

Then Alejandro looked disappointed. "Wait, is Lola home?"

"No. Her house is empty but she already said I could stay there.

She gave me the code for the garage."

He frowned but he didn't say anything. I couldn't interpret that look. Instead he turned to Olivia and Wester. "Sorry to interrupt your night. Thanks for coming out here, guys."

"Hey, no problem, man. And I'm swiping your chicken." Wester bent over the coffee table and grabbed a chicken leg. "Nice to meet you, Miranda."

"Nice to meet you, too." I smiled at Olivia. "Enjoy the rest of your night."

She gave me a smile in return. "I'm off the hook for entertaining Wester now that you gave him chicken."

"Wait, what?" Wester shook his head. "That is not how that works."

We all laughed and said our goodbyes. I locked the door after they left and faced Alejandro in the chaos of the boxes and the take-out food. "Your friends are nice. I feel bad they came over here and the conclusion is basically get out for now." I bit my lip. "Am I overreacting? Should I just stay here? I can sleep on the mattress on the floor and get this place together better tomorrow."

It was just part of my DNA to not want to make waves. I have a terrible habit of talking myself out of what my gut says.

"If you have a place to stay then why would you stay here feeling nervous? You'll never get a good night's sleep."

He had a point. It reassured me. I hated that I did that. I knew something was off next door, just like I had known something was off with Max.

I nodded. "Let me just pack a bag."

I started past him but he grabbed my hand and massaged my fingers. His eyes drifted to my lips. "I'm staying overnight with you."

Making a point of glancing down at his hand holding mine I said, "Oh, really? Do I have a choice?" It was a token protest. I knew he was staying with me. I also knew that I wanted him to.

He shook his head. "Not in me staying over. But where I'm going to sleep."

So he was letting me decide whether we repeated our explosive sex or not. The sexual tension that bounced between us still piqued my interest. We were standing there, staring at each other, and I could taste him on my lips, feel the press of his cock inside me. I hadn't expected to be attracted to him. I hadn't expected when I asked for a baby, I would want to give in to his demand that it be old school, skin on skin. But I did. I wanted him again and again.

More than any man in a very long time. He wanted me too and I had no doubt he could satisfy me all night long. He was a ladies' man and he had already proved he knew his way around a woman's body.

Besides, I had secrets that I couldn't reveal to Alejandro. If he knew everything there was to know, he would not be willing to help me start a family.

He would walk away and I would be forced to use a sperm bank.

I could do that. There was nothing wrong with some

anonymous sperm.

Or I could let this gorgeous man sweep me off my feet repeatedly over the next few weeks and give me some of his beautiful Cuban genes.

Sex was not something I had been expecting. But now that it was on the table, I couldn't resist taking more. Hell, this might be it for me for years.

"I know earlier was impulsive," I said. "But I accept your conditions," I told him. "And you can share my bed tonight. And again when it's time." I meant ovulation.

But Alejandro just gave me a slow smile. "I want thirty days. A full cycle."

My jaw dropped and my inner thighs went damp, simultaneously. He had some damn nerve. Yet I couldn't deny that it was sexy as hell, his confidence. But more importantly, the way he wanted me. He could have any woman. He didn't need me to warm his bed for a month, yet he wanted me to. The thought was very arousing.

"One, you have cojones like no one else." He didn't give much reaction so I continued. "Two, I know when I ovulate. It's science. We don't need thirty days."

Alejandro brought my hand to his mouth and drew the tip of my index finger into his mouth and sucked gently. Then he kissed each tip slowly, sensually. "It's called practice. But mostly just because I want to. I'm going to work at making you scream over and over and over, until you don't ever want me to stop."

My nipples hardened. Until I never stopped? What did that mean? He wanted more than sex?

I was going to agree though. I already knew that. I couldn't resist him. "You better make it worth my time."

When he looked at me I didn't see a guy who was younger than me. I saw an alpha, confident, sexual savant who knew he had me right where he wanted me. "Miranda. Don't insult me. You should never rush a good thing."

"I'll clear my calendar." I clung to a little bit of attitude to try and regain some kind of control, but I was well aware he very firmly had the upper hand on me.

He laughed softly. "I plan on clearing your mind, beautiful. And blowing it."

Suddenly I couldn't wait to be at his total mercy.

YOU KNOW WHEN you were a kid and it was Christmas morning and you opened up that one thing you'd been dying to get all damn year?

That's how I felt going in Lola Brandy's house with Miranda.

She was my fucking present and I was finally getting to unwrap her. If earlier had been any indication of how much I would enjoy it, I was in for the best night of my life. Plus twenty-nine additional nights. I honestly could not believe Miranda had agreed to my terms. Every night. Her naked. My cock inside her. *Damn.*

I was going to take it slowly and savor every second of it.

After I checked Miranda's place for any video or audio surveillance planted and was fairly certain it was clean, we headed over to Lola Brandy's house.

It was a typical property for the area. Low slung, with a Spanish influence, it had been remodeled at some point into a more modern glass box. I could smell the water so even though it was dark I knew her property backed up to the Intracoastal. It wasn't a massive house or lot at all. More of a pimped-up bungalow, unlike the twenty plus million dollar houses out on the islands. Like Ricardo Davis's place, Olivia's brother-in-law. This was not extravagant for a pop star. Lola Brandy got points in my book for spending conservatively.

You know, three million instead of twenty. The thought made me grin as Miranda used the keypad and sent the garage door sailing softly up.

"Nice place," I commented. "I wouldn't object to living on the water."

Miranda nodded. "It is a cool house. Plus there is a dock out back. She had a yacht but wasn't using it enough to justify it, so it's this eerie empty spot on the water now."

"Well, at least she doesn't keep stuff she doesn't need. A financially conservative pop star. Who knew there was such a thing?" We went through the garage and entered a door with another keypad code. It led to a mud room, and beyond that was the kitchen.

It was the Miami kitchen classic. White on white on white. Everything shiny and lacquered and crisp. The lights came on automatically when Miranda moved forward and I questioned that little electronic feature. Did I really want the lights to snap on every time I went into the kitchen at night? Sometimes I wanted a midnight snack without the floodlights dilating my pupils.

But I wasn't a rich guy. Maybe rich people liked to be slapped awake.

Miranda had packed a small bag. I had nothing with me obviously but I didn't need anything but her naked anyway. She set the bag on the kitchen counter and turned, leaning back against it. She looked nervous and curious and sexy as hell. "The guest room is the first door on the left. Lola's only request is that no one stays in her master bedroom."

"She's smart to keep her room off-limits." I gave her a smile. "Because what I'm going to do to you is filthy."

For being a woman who had traveled all over the country and the world, mingling with the rich and famous, Miranda had maintained a sweet innocence. She blushed at my words, despite what had gone down between us already. I wondered how many men she had dated in the years since Max disappeared and then decided that was an irrelevant thought. Whoever they had been they weren't around now. Only I was.

"Is that a promise or a threat?" she asked.

"Both."

She studied me for a second, a slight smile teasing across her lips. I wanted to cross the room, bite that plump skin and tug her against me. But I also wanted to draw the moment of anticipation out. "Do you want a drink? I can run out and get some wine."

"I'm sure there is something here. The house is usually pretty well stocked." Miranda went and opened the fridge. It was filled with sparkling water, juice, and white wine. "No beer though."

"Do you like wine?" I came up behind her and pressed my body against hers. I reached around her and pulled out a bottle. It was crisp and cold and I pressed the chilled glass against her arm.

She jerked a little but didn't totally pull away. "Yes. Should we have a toast?"

I lifted the hair at the back of her neck and gave her a soft kiss. She shivered. "Yes, we should toast," I said. "To forgetting about the shit from the past and grabbing the future."

Miranda turned. "Well, wait until we have glasses before you give the actual toast. And let's go outside on the patio."

She had a point. "I'll get some glasses." It was an easy kitchen to maneuver around in. There was zero clutter. The cabinets were filled with white dinnerware and clear stemware. It only took me opening three cabinets to find a dozen or so wine glasses carefully lined up. I pulled out two and righted them on the sparkly white countertop. Then I started digging around for a corkscrew.

Miranda bent over the countertop, propping her chin up, her hair falling over her arm, and her shirt gaping so that I got an amazing view of her tits. Full and creamy and begging for attention. "I can see down your shirt," I told her.

"I know. That's why I bent over."

That made me laugh. "You're full of surprises, aren't you? I can honestly say I didn't see that coming. You've been playing coy. Of course I didn't see that coming any more than I saw you saying you want a baby."

I wanted to touch her but I resisted. This was time to watch her. To learn her movements, her body language.

She just studied me as I kept searching. "I would say I'm sorry for springing that on you but really, what other way is there to do it? I thought about it a lot and then I just blurted it out."

"You're so domestic I would have thought you'd send me one of those damn packages people do for weddings now. Like butterflies emerging out of a box that says 'Will you be my baby daddy?'"

She laughed. "That sounds horrible!"

Finally I found the elusive corkscrew and pulled it out. "I got one for my buddy's wedding. His wife was behind that shit, she had to be. Because I'm telling you, Laurence would not have sent me a box of golf tees and some freaking card that said 'Let's tee off for my wedding' or whatever the hell it said."

"Maybe that works more for bridesmaids, you know, the whole elaborate presentation. Because if someone sent me a box of bath salts and a note, I would be touched."

"Maybe just send me the golf tees and then ask me later. Or ask me then give me a dude gift at the bachelor party." I opened the wine bottle with a pull.

"So what would a baby daddy box look like? Was I supposed to send you Viagra?" she teased.

I gave her a sharp look. "Fuck no. I don't need that. You know that." I knew she was just messing with me, but damn, that was insulting.

"Settle down," she said, watching me pour the wine. "It was a joke, big guy."

"It just gives me more reason to prove myself to you." I handed her a full glass of wine. "And I'm assuming big guy is referring to my cock."

She raised the glass. "Of course."

That wasn't ego boosting enough for me. I took her free hand in mine, lacing our fingers together. Then I drew her hand across the length of my cock, which was hard from anticipation and our banter. I squeezed. "Good enough for you?"

Her eyes had widened. "Do you just walk around hard?"

"Only around you."

"If you're looking for compliments I don't think you need one from me. You know what you have."

It was true, guys know where they land on the scale of peewee to porn star and I knew I was packing a decent weapon. Her expression showed me she agreed. That didn't mean I didn't want some appreciation. "You can't throw me a bone?" I didn't even intend the pun and I didn't laugh. I just used her hand to squeeze my cock harder.

"Not bad," she murmured. "If you're into that sort of thing."

"I'm going to be in to you for damn sure."

Miranda started to move her hand up and down without my assistance and that was the greatest compliment. My body reacted and I got harder. "You're playing with gunfire there," I told her.

But she just smirked. "Why, are you going to shoot without warning?"

She had her sassy moments and I loved it. I brushed my thumb over her bottom lip and let her continue to stroke me. "Hardly. You could do this for hours and I would enjoy it without finishing. But I'm not about to let you have that much control."

I knew she would pull her hand back and she did. "Why do you want control?"

Because I wanted to hold on to total control until she had none.

Until she understood that it was going to be me and her. I wasn't going to share that with her yet though.

"Because if I only have you for a month, I want to make the most of it." I gestured to the patio. "Let's go outside."

Not moving, she held me in place, her hand still firmly on my cock. She stroked up and down and gave me a wicked smile. "You're overdressed for this party."

I stepped back and took a sip of wine. "Does this house have a pool?"

"Of course."

"Then I can undress outside. And then undress you." Miranda naked, in the pool, water sluicing all over her juicy curves?

I could die a happy man after witnessing that.

CHAPTER 9

Alejandro held the glass of wine back out to me after swallowing half of it. I took it from him wryly. "Don't you have a second glass? You don't need to steal my wine."

"I like taking what is yours." He gave me a smirk.

Honestly, I should put him in his place. I handed him the glass back and reached for the second glass and poured myself fresh wine. "I'm only willing to put up with you because I feel bad your chicken dinner was interrupted."

"I think for a woman who is so sweet and honest, that was a big fat fucking lie."

I put my lips to the glass and sipped. I was only planning on one glass since I was trying to conceive. His words made me feel guilty. I wasn't sure how sweet and honest I was. I had secrets that would infuriate him if he learned the truth. Secrets about Max that made me hesitate, doubt creeping in. Maybe it wasn't right to involve Alejandro in my life, my secrets. "I'm not as sweet as you think I am."

"I know you have a sexy side, that's true."

Turmoil swirled inside me. "That's not what I'm talking about."

"What are you talking about, baby?"

Nothing that mattered, I realized. I wasn't planning to have a relationship with Alejandro. He wasn't going to be my boyfriend, or an active father to my child. So it was irrelevant.

I settled on something that did matter. "Don't put me on a pedestal. That's all. I don't want you doing this because you think I'm perfect, because I'm not."

But he just ran his thumb down my cheek. "To me, you are perfect."

"And you're the one who is sweet." He was. I could see in his eyes the sweet teen boy I had known. But it was more than that.

Alejandro was looking at me in a way that I hadn't experienced in years. If I were honest, maybe ever. It was like he thought I was the moon and the stars and every sunset ever. Like it was a privilege to touch me. He had never been a man with a shortage of words but now he was doing his talking with his eyes. With his touch. It was the sexiest thing I had ever experienced.

He smoothed my hair back off my cheeks, cupping my flesh, and studying my face. His gaze swept over me and his eyes were lit with the fire of passion. He looked like I was the most beautiful woman he'd ever seen.

"What I am is the luckiest fucking guy on the planet."

What woman could resist that? Not me. "Sweet talk will get

you everywhere."

He gave me a soft kiss. "Good." His lips brushed over mine, as he invaded my space. This kiss was deeper, hotter.

I wrapped my arms around his neck so I could meet him halfway. His touch was electrifying. Each kiss grew more intense, and I was gripping him harder, wanting more, when he bit my bottom lip and pulled back entirely.

Disappointed, I wiped my lip, breathing hard.

"Show me this pool," he said casually. "I think I need to cool off."

I glanced down at his cock. That thing wasn't going anywhere. It seemed crazy to me that he didn't want to just have me go at it. I was personally on board with a kitchen countertop moment. But what I was finding about Alejandro was he always had a plan.

"This way." I grabbed my wine glass and headed through the living room toward the sliders that led to the back patio. The pool was small but it had beautiful lighting and a dense row of foliage on either side of the property to prevent a view of the neighbors' houses.

Given that it was April, it was almost a guarantee to be a beautiful night and it didn't disappoint. We hadn't seen rain in days and it was warm, with a balmy breeze off the water. I breathed in the smell of the water. "Best thing about being home is definitely the water."

"And here I thought the best thing about being home was us."

Warning bells clamored in the back of my head. "There isn't

an us," I said, gently, wanting to remind him of the reality of what I was asking.

He didn't look offended or mulish. He just looked amused, like he thought I was naïve as hell. He peeled his T-shirt off, revealing all those glorious muscles. He had a scar on his shoulder I hadn't noticed earlier. He sat down in a chaise and I dropped into the one beside him. "Where did you get that scar?" I asked, reaching out and tracing it with the tip of my finger.

"Believe it or not, tailgating at a Dolphins game. The wind blew our tent over and the metal support sliced me open like a fillet. It was a freak accident. Bled like crazy." He gave me a grin. "I usually say I got it in a knife fight. It sounds cooler."

That made me roll my eyes. "It's not like you tripped over your own feet and cut yourself on a palm tree or something. That would be embarrassing." I took another sip of the wine, then handed him the glass. "Here. You can finish this." I felt nervous again for some reason.

Which was ludicrous. But I forged ahead. "So what's the craziest assignment you've ever had as a bodyguard?"

"Crazy?" He shrugged, raising his knee and tapping it with his thumb. He drained my glass and set it down on the tile next to his glass. "This is Miami and I oversee the rich and famous. Everyone is crazy. Though I had one guy in particular who was about eighty years old and spent all day walking around his house completely naked. There was something both horrifying and awesome about that. I had to give the guy credit. He had no fucks to give, you know?"

"I never thought of myself as someone who cared what other people thought, but I am old enough now and introspective enough to realize that's not true. I do care what people think. Is that bad?"

But Alejandro shook his head slowly. "No, that's not bad. Being a person who thinks about how their actions will affect others is a good thing, Miranda. In a world of selfish human beings, you're a rare and beautiful soul."

There it was again. That look. Like I was something special and awe-inspiring. I couldn't live up to that adoration, but that didn't mean I couldn't enjoy it. I leaned toward him. "Will you please kiss me?" I whispered, my body aching with want that went far beyond arousal. He was digging in, creeping into my heart, and it was scary, but at the same time so compelling.

"I thought you'd never ask."

His hand snaked out and buried in my hair and he moved closer, closer, eyes locked on me. I sighed without meaning to, but wanting to remember this moment. Then his mouth covered mine and I closed my eyes, needing to hide from the enormity of what I was feeling. I focused on the feel of him. The soft brush of our lips, the smell of his cologne, the hard plane of his chest. I ran my fingers over his bare flesh, greedy.

When his tongue coaxed my lips open I gave in willingly, wanting him to sweep inside me, dominate me. He didn't disappoint. While his mouth did delicious things to me, his hand lowered, caressing my skin from my neck down to the swell of my breast. He cupped the tender flesh, like he was testing the weight of my breast. Then his thumb brushed over my nipple through the fabric of my cotton shirt.

He made a sound of impatience and pulled back. Then he yanked my shirt over my head. My hair covered my eyes then tumbled over my shoulders. He was eyeing my chest with naked desire. "Come here." He took my hand and pulled me forward to the end of the chaise.

Alejandro stood up and raised me to my feet. "What are we doing?" I murmured.

"Skinny dipping." He reached behind my back and unlatched my bra. It sprang forward, slipping down my shoulders.

"My turn." I undid the snap on his shorts and slid the zipper down. I couldn't resist reaching inside and stroking his erection through the fabric of his boxer briefs. Just the feel of the pulsating bulge made my mouth water. I wanted to suck him, to take him deep, and make him lose that smirk. I wanted him raw and desperate.

But I wasn't going on my knees on the tile. I had a better idea.

He kissed me again, while I continued to work on his cock with my palm. Then he was tugging on my pants, forcing them down. "Need help?" I asked.

"Why are these so damn tight? They look fantastic on you, but are a serious cock block," he asked. "But I don't need help, thanks. I refuse to give up. It's my right to get you naked."

I wasn't sure that it was but I wasn't going to argue with him. "You're very stubborn."

"No. It's called intensity."

Whatever it was, he had my pants down to my ankles. I stepped out of them. Alejandro slipped my bra straps down my arms and tossed the bra back onto the chaise.

Then he bent over and drew my nipple into his mouth and I gripped his biceps, shocked at how amazing such a simple touch felt. It had been too long since I had experienced this kind of easy desire. I felt like I had been working at it for years, making it happen. This was effortless. I moaned in disappointment when he stepped away. I had felt his cock with my hands, with my body, but I hadn't really had the opportunity to study Alejandro naked. He was gorgeous. Every inch the charming and sexy man, his body hard and strong.

My hair was tumbling down over my breasts and I felt decadent being outside. The warm breeze was teasing my nipples to taut peaks. "This feels very naughty being outside naked," I said.

"It's about to get naughtier."

I had no doubt.

I wasn't known for naughty. Despite the fact that I had made a career out of both dancing and as a body double in next to zero clothing, I was a modest person. Max didn't want me to be a porn star and since then, the men I had been with had been casual relationships and I wasn't comfortable enough to be totally uninhibited. So here I was standing, thirty freaking years old, and I couldn't say that I had experienced naughty in the truest sense of the word. It wasn't that I hadn't wanted to or wasn't capable of it, I just hadn't had the opportunity.

Here was my chance. With Alejandro.

I trusted him.

So I stood there in my panties and heels and let both the breeze and Alejandro kiss my bare skin. When he pinched both of my nipples simultaneously, I gasped. "What was that for?"

"Because it feels good, doesn't it?"

It did. He was kissing my neck and his grip tightened, rolling my sensitive flesh through his fingers.

I felt it straight in my womb and a rush of warmth was between my thighs. It hurt yet in the best way possible. I felt ridiculously naïve and uncertain, knowing that my sexual education had some serious gaps in it. There was nothing I could do except stand there and let him take the lead. Let him dominate the situation and me. Because he was good at it. He had a path he wanted to walk me down and I was willing.

"There's music out here," I said, voice breathy and nervous, as he pulled my earlobe between his teeth and bit at the same time he squeezed my nipples yet again. "Oh geez," I blurted, without meaning to.

"Oh geez, there's music? Is that what you mean?" he murmured. "Because I don't hear any music. Or was it oh geez, that feels good, Alejandro, never stop?"

"I meant it feels good. But if you want music I can turn it on." I felt the need to play hostess. It was ingrained in me, the desire to make others comfortable. It was because I was craving a home so much. I was envisioning having friends over, entertaining, making appetizers that everyone would love.

But right now I was stupidly nervous and I defaulted to trying to be accommodating. I stepped back. I was the one who needed the damn music. I needed to calm the hell down. "I'll go put it on."

For some reason I expected him to stop me. Or maybe I wanted him to stop me. To distract me from my own anxiety. But he didn't. He just watched me walk over to the outdoor kitchen where there was an iPad in the drawer to work all the lights and music. I had to bend over but once the slow nineties music was playing softly from all corners of the yard, I stood there mostly naked and took a deep bracing breath. I could do this.

It was like owning the stage when I danced. It didn't matter that the only thing I was wearing was panties and heels. If I had a bikini top on it would be like half the time at work. The difference was though that I didn't want to play a part. I wanted to be me. The real Miranda. Not a dancer or a body double but just me. A woman who was stealing a few minutes with her man.

Except he wasn't my man.

Hence the damn nerves.

But I thought about Alejandro inside me. The way his touch drove me wild. I felt my breasts grow heavy, my body tense and tight with need. This was me. This was me wanting him to fuck me hot and hard. This was me wanting to finally, for the first time, know what it meant to be a naughty girl.

So I strolled across the tile beside the pool. I had a tremendous amount of experience walking in heels and getting myself out of heels. My initial thought was to stroll up to Alejandro but I changed my mind and dropped down onto the ground by the edge of the pool. Knees up, I undid the straps of my heels first one, then the other. I slipped them off and glanced up, sensing Alejandro on the move.

Before he could influence what I was about to do, I stood back up and shimmied out of my panties. He made a sound deep in his throat. "Sit down," I told him.

I did so myself and dangled my feet into the water. It was a perfect temperature. Refreshing but not cold. "Ah," I said, tossing my hair back and arching my back so that my breasts were displayed to full advantage.

"You're killing me," he said, sitting down beside me. "Is the water cold?"

"No." I slipped down into it, using my arms. Then I bounced on my tiptoes and maneuvered myself between his legs.

His eyebrows went up. "What is going on here?"

"I'm just finding a more comfortable position." With that, I gripped the base of his shaft and took the full length of his thick cock into my mouth.

MIRANDA HAD A way of shocking me. First seeing her holding a knife. Then a gun. It was at odds with what I knew about her.

But taking the initiative and sucking me? Totally fine by me, even if it was unexpected. She had the sweetest mouth and right now she was very enthusiastically going down on me. Watching her blond head bent over me, her tits bobbing in the pool, I felt that draw deep down into my balls and everything tightened. She was gorgeous and this was a fantasy come true.

I stroked her hair, overwhelmed by both tenderness and the urgent need to pound her mouth with my cock.

Settling for somewhere in between, I gripped her hair and encouraged her. "That's it, baby. That feels amazing."

Glancing up as she pulled fully back, she shot me a smile. It was the hottest fucking view I had ever had. I tugged harder on her blond strands, unable to resist. "Get back on there," I told her, hearing how raw and gravely my voice sounded.

I was hanging on to my control by a thread. What I really wanted to do was take over, thrust into her. But I gritted my teeth and waited for her.

"Something tells me you like this," she said.

"You could say that." It was instinct to close my eyes, but there was no way I wanted to miss this view.

"How's this?" She flicked her tongue over the tip.

I shrugged, amused by her flirtatious little smile. "It's a tease."

"Oh, so you want this?" She wrapped her lips around and sucked, drawing me halfway.

"Yes, I want this. I want it deep."

Suddenly she gave it to me. I was fully engorged in her hot

little mouth and I felt my balls tighten. I groaned without meaning to. I wanted to stay in control but I couldn't help but express my pleasure at her very naked enthusiasm towards my cock. She was going hard on me now, finding a fast, hot rhythm that created a slick heat.

"That's it, baby. You're doing beautiful."

I let myself enjoy her, but held on tight to my control, my body tense. My jaw was set and my knuckles were white, gripping her shoulders. Every time she slid her warm mouth down to the base of my shaft, I felt it to the base of my balls and all the way down to my toes.

But then she shifted and her breasts bobbed above the water, brushing against my thighs, wet and warm and full. It was too much and I didn't want to deny myself her pussy. I needed her pussy.

So I yanked her back off of me. She looked up at me, surprised, making a little sound of pleasure as she wiped her swollen lips. Holy shit, she was stunning. The ends of her hair had been soaked with pool water and clung to her dewy flesh. Her nipples were a dusky pink and tight, water droplets rolling down her breasts. Her eyes were bright and wide, dark with lust. The corner of her mouth was turned up, like she was pleased with herself and her performance, as she should be.

"What's wrong?" she asked. "Not deep enough? I can try harder." She was resting on my knees, the water giving her enough buoyancy that I wasn't concerned she was straining.

Her words nearly killed me. "You sexy little flirt. You know full well you had my cock as far back in your throat as it can go and that I fucking loved it."

Miranda gave a little laugh. "Maybe. But there's nothing to say I can't try."

I almost gave in. I almost let her take me back into her mouth and fuck me with those sweet lips until I came.

But I resisted. That could come another day. I had thirty. No sense in rushing anything. "Get up here." I pulled her up out of the water by her forearms.

She squawked. "Alejandro! Stop."

"Why? I want you closer to me." I got her into my lap, her skin cool from the pool. Water splattered over me as we collided, skin on damp skin. Goose bumps rose on her flesh. "Mmm, this is better." She was all juicy curves and plump lips.

Her knees were bent so she could rest in my lap facing me. "Hi," she whispered.

"Hi." I reached down and stroked between her folds. Miranda sighed. "What's this?" I asked. "I found something wet that I want."

"How do you want it?" She shook her head a little in an attempt to get her hair back off of her shoulders, but it clung there, damp.

"That's a loaded question." I sank my thumb into her body. "I want it every single way possible." I kissed her. "But for now I want it wrapped around my cock just like this. I want you to lift yourself up just a little so I can fuck you. Can you do that, baby?"

She nodded eagerly. "Uh-huh." She made little sounds of

excitement in the back of her throat as she raised up her ass, all while I continued to tease at her clit with her own moisture.

I wondered if she knew how much she looked like an old-school porn star. She was a breathy seventies goddess, all full hips and big tits, teased-up blond hair, and wide doe-eyed innocence. It was unbelievable. She had the most amazing combination of a killer body and a sweet heart that made it seem like an act, even when she was either groaning with pleasure or seeming totally startled by how good it felt.

All I knew for sure was that I was one lucky son of a bitch because most men would give their right arm for a woman this damn hot sitting herself down onto their cock.

When her body connected with mine, her hands gripping my biceps, I lost all ability to think. I could only feel. And what I felt was the most intense ecstasy I had ever experienced.

CHAPTER
10

"Are you okay?" I asked Miranda, despite my deep need to take her hard. "You're not getting scraped on the tile, are you?"

"No. All I feel is you." Her head had fallen back, her breasts deliciously close to my mouth.

"Let me know if we need to move to the furniture." I drew her nipple between my lips. "I don't want you to get hurt."

"Why, is it going to get rough?"

"You tell me. You're the one steering this ship right now." She was moving slowly, rolling her hips, giving me the ultimate lap dance. "You seem to know what you're doing."

"I have good thigh strength," she murmured. "I am willing to put it to good use."

Her skin was soft, yet toned. The water rolled from her body down over my thighs, my arms, where she gripped my biceps. The goose bumps on her shoulders had me reaching and flicking my tongue over the cool skin. "I'm very appreciative of that fact."

There was no way she had any idea how gorgeous she was. I was having a sense that I was in a dream, one of blue lights, shimmering pool water, her creamy naked flesh, and me, yet at the same time nothing had ever felt more real. I could taste and touch and smell every inch of her, and I let her leisurely ride my cock while I absorbed every sensation that I could. I was going to hold on to this, to the feel of her. I gripped her ass, wanting to explore every single one of her delicious curves.

"Alejandro?" she asked, rising way up so that only the tip of my cock was still inside her.

I gritted my teeth, wanting to just grab her hips and slam her back down. "Yeah, baby?"

"I can't get it deep enough," she breathed, before dropping back down onto me.

That was it. There was nothing sexier than that and if she wanted it deep, I was going to give her just that. Even when she squeezed down onto me, it was like we weren't close enough. Even with her body in my lap, both of us gripping the other, it wasn't enough skin on skin, the slap of pleasure that I was craving and clearly she was too. "Hold on, we're going to stand up."

"What? How?"

My feet were still in the water and I drew them out. "Just wrap your hands around my neck and hold on." This was why I sweated in the gym day after day. So I could look like a badass fucking my girl. I held on to her and stood up with barely a grunt while she gave a cry of surprise.

"Oh my," she said. "Be careful."

"I got it." I had her and damn, I did not want to let her go. All I wanted to do was keep a tight grip on Miranda forever. I lifted her leg up high on my waist and carried her to the outdoor kitchen and settled her on the countertop.

She jumped. "Damn, that's cold."

"Don't worry, I'll warm you up." I drew her knees up and her feet rested on the front of my thighs.

Instinctively she tried to close her legs a bit but I paused her action. "Uh-uh. No hiding from me."

She tossed her hair back and pushed her chest forward. "I'm not hiding. It's just awkward. I'm on a concrete slab."

For some reason that pissed me off. It was like she didn't think I was good enough. It brought to mind the reason she was here with me—not because she was my girlfriend but because she wanted my damn sperm. Sure, I could make her come but she still had an ulterior motive.

It had been a long day and she might have her own reasons but she wanted this just as much as I did.

"Should I take you to a bed? Is that what you want? You want it pretty and sweet and full of rose petals?" My voice was soft, a smile fixed on my face.

She stilled. "What is that supposed to mean?"

I almost spoke again, ruining it further. But I stopped myself.

I was making too much out of it. The countertop was cold and hard, what the fuck did I expect? It was only hours from the first time we'd had sex. The shift in our relationship was intimate but startling. The last thing she needed was me being a dick.

Instead of saying anything I just leaned in and kissed her, hard, my fingers finding their way between her thighs into her damp pussy.

Miranda gave a cry of pleasure.

Feeling impatient and on edge, I went straight for two fingers, enjoying the way her body arched toward my touch, her little gasp of shock and delight ringing in my ears. I was in dangerous territory and I knew it. I had wanted this woman for a decade and now I had her and I felt possessive, eager, almost angry. I wanted to imprint on her, make it so she could never forget this. I wanted to be tender and loving and demanding and greedy all at once.

"You like that?" I asked, drinking in the sight of her spread out for me, skin still damp in places from the pool, her hair starting to dry in frizzy little ringlets. It was wild and wanton and I loved everything about what I saw. She was the ultimate Venus goddess to me, the epitome of feminine sexuality and beauty.

"Yes." She didn't embellish any further, though her eyes drifted shut.

I concentrated on massaging her in to a deep, boneless pleasure, listening to her body, to her reaction to each stroke of my fingers, each tease and slide. The moisture from her pussy soaked me as I sank inside her over and over, wanting to draw it out, and drive her insane.

She looked so beautiful, so delicious, that I couldn't resist. I bent over and stroked my tongue over her sweetness. "Baby, you taste so good."

"Oh, I can't, you need to stop." She was arching her back and yanking on my hair. "I'm going to come."

"So come." I didn't break my rhythm at all.

But Miranda shoved me away. "Take me to the couch, the bed, somewhere."

I really wanted to put her on her feet, turn her around and take her from behind, but even more than that I wanted to stare into her eyes as I took her over the edge. I didn't want to waste one second of my time with Miranda. "You got it, baby."

Scooping her off the countertop into my arms I took her across the patio and through the open glass doors. The house was hushed, cool compared to poolside. The music was still faintly audible, but it was more that I could feel the pulse of the R&B music than actual notes or lyrics. The air conditioning was set to a cooler temperature than I would have preferred so after I laid Miranda down on the sofa, I pulled a soft fuzzy blanket off the arm and draped it over her skin. "You look cold," I explained.

There were goose bumps on her arms still.

"I forgot to towel off after swimming."

After sucking my cock. The memory made me hard all over again. She was amazing. "Sorry, I shouldn't have put you on that cold countertop."

"You can get under here with me and warm me up." Miranda reached out for me.

It still felt unreal that she would be reaching for me. I needed to get over the feeling that it was a fucking dream that would disappear if I closed my eyes for more than a split second. "I've never wanted anything more than to warm you up."

Sliding under the blanket, I took a minute to pull Miranda to me, to hold her. To feel the length of her curvaceous body pressed up against mine.

"Mm," she said. "You're warm."

Snuggling in along side of me, she wrapped her hands around my waist. Her head fit into the crook of my arm. Damn, this felt good. The tenderness almost overtook my desire. Almost. Having her skin against mine caused my erection to grow harder against her thigh. But I wanted a minute to just hold her, enjoy the closeness. The intimacy.

This way I could almost imagine that we had fast-forwarded into the future and this was real. Miranda as my wife.

Then I shoved the thought away. That was stupid, allowing myself a fantasy. It didn't matter what happened tomorrow, six months from now, a year down the line. What mattered was right here, right now. So I shifted so that I rose overtop of her and I kissed her soft lips. I allowed my eyes to drift closed and I committed this to memory. The feel of her lithe fingers on my back, her breasts brushing my chest. Her feet sliding along the backs of my calves. The smell of her skin, like chlorine and flowers, the musk of her arousal. The view of her raspberry lips, her amber eyes shining with desire, and something else. A tenderness. She cared about me. That was never in question.

I felt as in the moment as it was possible and as I kissed her, I drank in all those sensations and appreciated each and every second of her. Her tongue tangled with mine hotly and she grew restless, shifting her legs, arching her hips so that she repeatedly bumped against my cock. Still I did nothing more. I just kissed and kissed, like we were sixteen and there was no other end game besides making out. My body started to burn and I tossed the blanket on the floor, our passion heating up between us.

When I pushed inside her, I never wanted to leave.

She was going to have to kick me out.

WHEN I CAME staring up at Alejandro, moving over me slowly and with amazing skill and strength, I felt something inside me shatter. He had taken me rough, fast, hard, and now tenderly. I couldn't protect myself from any of it. I couldn't protect myself from him.

I was being dragged under by the current and even while I knew I could drown, I didn't even try to escape. I wanted Alejandro to pull me under and make me forget everything that ever was and ever would be. I wanted to let go of the past and embrace the here and now.

His eyes were dark as night and his expression was fierce, yet sweet. That was Alejandro. Sweet but fierce. Which to me, was the perfect man.

My back arched as I gave in and let him milk the deepest shattering pleasure from me.

His hand slid under my ass and he raised me up so that he could take me deeper, until I wasn't sure where he ended and I began. Until I was on the verge of losing myself entirely in his overwhelming passion.

Until I felt a tear slide down my cheek. I don't know why. Or where it came from. I only knew that an earthquake had shifted the ground beneath my feet.

"Oh my God, don't cry," he murmured, bending down to kiss the droplet away. "Should I stop?"

"No. Never." I shook my head and gripped him tighter, wanting to keep him inside me.

"Never," he agreed.

He exploded inside me, and then he stared down at me, breathing hard.

We fell asleep in each other's arms, bodies still connected in the most primal way possible.

The next night I hummed in the kitchen of my rental as I unpacked, making serious headway on the boxes. Because I wanted to start cooking, exploring new recipes, and working on my knife skills before school started, it was important to me to get this room together first. Alejandro was installing a security system and I paused when I saw him move past my sight line. It brought a smile to my face.

He was very sweet and very, very sexy. He noticed me watching him and he gave me a wink. Damn it, I blushed. Like a teen girl. But I couldn't prevent the heat from blooming across my cheeks. The night before had been so damn hot. The things he had done to me... I had the sore body to prove it. But I was sore in the best, most satisfied way possible.

The house felt hopeful again to me in daylight. I felt like maybe I had been paranoid the night before, too quick to be concerned. Max the cat was lying on an unopened box, grooming himself with supreme nonchalance.

Maybe the man next door was just weird. There were plenty of odd characters in Miami. It didn't mean he was malicious in any way. And plenty of cats were named Max. That was just pure coincidence.

Once I was done unpacking my kitchen I was going to run to Publix and stock up on food. I was feeling the very instinctive and feminine need to feed Alejandro. I also needed to get cat food.

Alejandro had some sort of electronic equipment in his hand but he took the few steps toward me and gave me a soft kiss. "Hi."

"Hi." I had a saucepan in my hand so I couldn't wrap my arms around his neck the way I wanted to. "Everything going okay?"

"Yes, ma'am."

Max jumped from the box to the counter and meowed, rubbing against my arm. "I think he's jealous of you."

"He should be." Even as he said it though Alejandro reached out and scratched the cat's head and ears. "Shouldn't you try to figure out who this guy belongs to? We can't just keep him."

The use of the term "we" both terrified and thrilled me. I didn't think he had even realized he'd used it, or that he actually meant anything by it. But all I knew that eighteen hours ago I hadn't known what I knew now—that there could be a we if I allowed it. I knew the second my eyes had opened that morning, Alejandro warm and rock solid and sexy beside me, that thirty days was his way of making his case. That he wanted to be with me. And that it was my decision. One word and this could be real life.

Me and Alejandro, a home, a cat, a baby.

It made me feel almost faint.

I wasn't even sure why it scared me so much.

Maybe it was because I had unfinished business with his brother and I didn't know how to fix that.

I also had secrets Alejandro wouldn't like.

So I had to stay strong. I couldn't tumble into a relationship. In to love.

"We did try to find his owner. We called the number on his collar. What else are we supposed to do?"

"Call the APL or something."

I shrugged. "I guess, but I mean, it's not my fault the information on his tag is wrong."

"Don't you care that someone might be looking for him, and is worried?"

"Sure. I have sympathy for anyone missing someone." There was a hell of a lot of truth to that.

Alejandro realized the undertone and snorted, rolling his eyes. It shattered the mood.

"But like I said, what am I supposed to do?" I asked. I felt defensive about the cat. The way I did about Max.

Damn it, I hated the low-level tension that raced along the edges of everything we did and said. Max was the white elephant in the room and trying to have an intimate relationship with that ominous shadow over us was putting me on edge, even in the best moments. This was why I hadn't wanted to have sex with Alejandro. This was why I had wanted him to go to the fertility clinic and keep it clinical, efficient.

This was messy.

But would I give it back now if I could? I seriously doubted it. There was something too electric between us. Too amazing.

There was a giant unspoken question between us but neither of us broke the silence with the words that would destroy everything. I knew what he was thinking, even though his expression was enigmatic. Would I be with Max if he reappeared?

It wasn't a fair question to ask though and that's why I was relieved he didn't. I couldn't answer that. Not when I didn't know if it would ever be reality or not.

"What do you want for dinner?" I asked. "I'm going to go to the store."

"You," he said gruffly, running his hand down my cheek. "That's all I want."

"You're going to get awfully hungry then," I said lightly, trying to ease the tension thick between us.

Alejandro shook his head. "I'm already hungry. I've been starving for a decade."

When he looked at me like that... arousal surged inside me, volcanic, urgent and hot and unexpected. "I want you to fuck me," I said, the words bursting out before I even fully knew I was thinking them.

Sex made everything else go away. It was just him and me.

He didn't answer me. He just took my shoulders and turned me quickly, shoving me against the wall. The movement spun my head and robbed me of breath. He had my sundress up around my stomach in a heartbeat and he tore off my panties by simply ripping the waistband so that they started a slow slide down my hips. Settling my calf on his hip he surged into me without a second wasted.

There against the ancient aqua tile of my retro kitchen he gave me what I wanted, over and over, a hard, fast pounding that overpowered all our wary side-stepping of unspoken truths. It was easier to focus on the ecstasy of the slick passage he took relentlessly. Our language was lust. We spoke with sex.

What was he telling me? I forced myself to keep my eyes open, to study his expression, his shuttered eyes.

His eyes spoke the words we never could—that I was his. That to him, I had always been his. And that by submitting to him, by taking the pleasure and the love he gave me, I owned that. Admitted I was his.

It was that thought that had me crying out, paired as it was with the deep thrust of his cock, lifting me up onto my toes with each push. I came hard, digging my nails into his shoulders, needing a grip. An anchor.

That was how it was with Alejandro. He destroyed me. But he was the one person in my life who would always be there to hold me up.

I could fall in love with him.

I wondered if I half had already.

He exploded inside me, his jaw clenched, expression fierce.

When he had slowed, he cupped my cheeks and kissed me. "What else do you need me to do for you today?" he asked softly, gently, like he hadn't just taken me hard against the wall. As if he wasn't even now still buried inside me, his warm seed tangling with my own moisture.

I shook my head, laughing breathlessly. "You've done plenty."

"Give you a baby?"

My breath caught. "Not today."

Alejandro seemed less than pleased with my answer. He pulled back, giving a sigh when our sticky bodies disengaged. "Let me know when you want it again. I'm here."

His words seemed mocking, but his tone was easy, casual. Like he was offering me a taste of his dessert. *You want another one? No? Are you sure?*

He always had a way of throwing me off kilter.

"You sound like a waiter."

Alejandro took another step back, adjusting his jeans. "I'm not a server. Or an employee. I'm your lover. I'm the man who loves you. You can do what you want with that, but don't joke about it."

My panties were around my ankles and my skirt was still bunched up around my hips. But I froze, shocked. "You're the one blackmailing me."

"You don't want this?" he asked.

I shook my head, feeling defiant. He was blackmailing me. He'd given me an ultimatum.

"Liar."

"Don't call me a liar!" I couldn't get those words out of my head. He was my lover. He was the man who loved me.

I wanted to just run and jump into his arms and throw caution to the wind and take that love and hold it close forever. But I was afraid.

Oh my God. I was afraid he would leave me. Just like Max had.

The thought made me catch my breath.

That was why I was holding back. That was why I was refusing to accept that the foundation of feelings for Alejandro could grow if I let them.

All these damn years of clinging to my relationship with Max was because I was afraid everyone was right. That he had left me.

"Maybe liar is the wrong way to put it. You're just not honest with yourself," he added.

Despite my revelation that still pissed me off. "What do you think my truth is?"

For some reason that made him grin. "That you want me."

"That's not something I've been dishonest about." I simultaneously wanted to end this conversation and resolve it. We were circling something, only I didn't know what. I shoved my skirt back down and stepped out of my ruined panties. I bent over and retrieved them to toss in the trash.

"You just shook your head a minute ago."

I scooped Max the cat off the counter. I really needed to change his name to something less emotionally charged. I held him against my chest and raked my fingers through his soft orange fur. Feeling the cat purr grounded me. "Alejandro. Are we making a mistake?"

"About what?"

Raising my gaze, I met his head on. "Us. Because we are creating an us, aren't we?"

His nostrils flared. "I'm trying to. But you have to tell me what you want. I'm going to ask you today and I'm going to ask you again in twenty-eight days. Other than that, I swear I won't bring it up."

The cat clawed at me to get down. I set him on the floor. I looked at Alejandro and I tried to listen to my heart. Not to my fear. Not to my ambitions to be a mother. But to my heart.

"What I want is you. And me. And a chance at a life together."

It was out and I couldn't take it back.

But he took me into his arms and murmured in my ear, "I love you."

And everything made sense with his strong shoulders there for me to lean on.

CHAPTER 11

"Sit down," Mickey told me. He was smoking a cigarette at his desk, which surprised me. I had never seen him smoke inside his office. "Wester told me you were looking for intel on your girl's rental. You could have come to me about that, you know."

"I didn't want to bother you." I had mixed feelings about Mickey and I had since I had started working for him four years earlier. I knew that he and Ryan had issues and I knew that Mickey skirted the law, and downright ran over moral boundaries, but at the same time, he had always been good to me. He had believed in me when I had been adrift, no clue what to do with my life, frustrated with my family, and feeling like I had lost any sense of purpose.

Mickey was the kind of man who didn't doubt himself. His confidence was boundless and that had served him well in business. He was also shrewd. So I trusted his assessment of any situation. "So we have a couple of things going on here." Mickey took another drag on his cigarette and rocked back in his chair.

I sat across from him and I waited, restless, running my palms down my thighs. I wasn't going to like whatever I was about to hear, I was convinced of it. "What's up?"

"So the house is a dead end. It's owned by some bullshit LLC that has only been around for two months and has no other transactions. I'm going to see who owns it but right now that information is hidden by a fake name that holds an additional LLC. So they have buried it a little, but there is always a way to get to the bottom of the hole."

I nodded. That sounded actually worse than what I was expecting. It meant my suspicions were on point. Something was off in that house. "What's your take on surveillance equipment being there?"

Mickey just shook his head. "No point in speculating."

It was hard not to do just that. I couldn't imagine what Miranda might be involved in. She hadn't even been in town for years. So I didn't think it had anything to do with her, which made it unnerving. I didn't want her to be collateral damage for something shady she wasn't even a part of. "So that's it?" I asked, and I realized I sounded impatient, frustrated.

Mickey dropped his cigarette onto the tile of his office floor and twisted his boot into it. There was still a cloud of smoke lingering in front of his face and I was slightly bewildered as to what the hell was going on with him but I wasn't stupid enough to ask.

"No, that's not it." Mickey shot me a wry look. "I found your brother. He's living in Texas on the Mexican border, working at a hotel. His name is Miguel Gonzalez and he spends a great deal of time with a well-known drug gang. He also crosses the border daily, claiming to be a Mexican citizen with a day visa to work in the US."

For a second, I wasn't even sure how to feel. I had known Max was alive. I was completely convinced of it. Yet hearing confirmation of that didn't give me the feeling of relief that I expected. I had thought that I would feel triumphant that Max was the manipulative piece of shit I had always known he was. Like hearing he was alive and just skipped would give me the proof I had always craved. All those years of everyone believing he was a charming guy and now I could say definitely that they were wrong.

Yet I just felt… flat. It didn't matter if people had ever believed me. It wasn't and had never been my job to go around warning everyone what an asshole Max was. His life was his to fuck up and the people he surrounded himself with now were most likely his evil counterparts. They didn't need a warning from me.

But Miranda. There was Miranda.

A week ago I would have given anything for her to admit that Max was not all Mr. Nice Guy and she had, although reluctantly. But now? After a full week of spending time with her, of loving both her body and her spirit, freely, without guilt, the last thing in the fucking world I wanted was for her to be hurt. Even if that meant I wouldn't be right.

"Any chance of him being on the move any time soon?"

"I doubt it. It looks like he's been there almost four years. He seems entrenched and since he is playing an illegal, he doesn't have much freedom of movement. He has to cross back over the border every night or lose his day visa."

"Except that once in the US, he can assume his real identity at any point and no one will be able to do anything about it, or hell, even be able to prove he was living as Miguel Gonzalez. There are only about a million guys with that name."

"That's true. Was he wanted as Max Garcia?"

"No. If he was, the cops would have been at my door right away." It didn't make any sense to me why Max would ditch out on everything in order to live the life of a day laborer in Mexico and Texas. There was no heat on him in Miami that I knew of and if he wanted to tell Miranda and my parents to fuck off he could have. I seriously doubted that any sense of guilt would have sent him fleeing versus just being honest about his lack of interest in a further relationship. "Are you sure you have the right guy?"

Something was off. Max wasn't known for being a hard worker.

Mickey shot me a look. "You doubting me?"

"No, I just don't think my brother would be cool working as a grunt. It's not his style."

"Then I would say he's hiding from something. The question is, what?"

That was the million-dollar question. "I have no idea."

"By the way, I looked into your girl."

That made me frown. "Why? I didn't ask you to do that."

"I had to. She was connected to him. Looking for him meant looking into her."

A niggle of concern made my chest tighten. I didn't want my fantasy shattered. Though I couldn't imagine what he would tell me that I didn't already know. Miranda was genuine in her belief that Max was dead. "And?"

"There was some kind of incident where a gun was fired... drugs all around. But there were no charges filed."

"Drugs? That can't be right. Miranda doesn't do drugs." That seriously bewildered me. "Possession? It must have been my brother's stuff."

"Someone broke in, presumably to steal the drugs, but Miranda fired at them. The reports are very vague but for whatever reason no charges were filed against Miranda."

I had no clue what to make of that. It seemed to me like my brother's dirty hands were all over the situation. But it made me wonder what Max was doing and what exactly Miranda knew.

The image of her with a gun in her hand popped into my head. She had looked awfully comfortable.

I was in love with Miranda.

But now I was wondering who the hell Miranda really was.

MAKING SMOKED MAHI with a pineapple chutney, I was checking the sear on the fish when I heard it again—a weird clicking noise from the unit next door. I wasn't sure if it was my imagination, or if there really were unexplained sounds emanating from the other side of our shared wall, but it seemed like every day there was something that set me on edge.

I hated it.

Everything else in my life was perfection. I didn't start classes until the summer session so I had time to kill during the day. I had gotten a part-time job at a restaurant, figuring I needed to learn to take the heat of an actual kitchen, as opposed to cooking just for myself and Alejandro. So far it was educational and everyone was friendly.

And Alejandro.

We were barely in to his thirty days and I knew beyond a shadow of a doubt that I was falling in love with him. He was the most bewildering combination of sweet and forceful. He had a tenderness that made me melt. I knew I was skating on thin ice but I also knew I couldn't resist him. There was no way I could cut our time together short, not when every moment was fun. He made me laugh, he made me feel beautiful. He made my body do things I hadn't even known it was capable of.

I also knew that I would be pregnant by the end of the month. It felt destined to happen. The thought gave me all the feels. All the warm and fuzzy and loving thoughts and sometimes I wondered if Alejandro might want to stick around.

But the only thing interrupting all my unexpected bliss was the weird lingering feeling that something next door was off, and that it involved me.

So turning the stove burner off, I decided that enough was enough. I was going to make someone answer the damn door if I had to pound on it all night. If the dinner I was making for Alejandro got ruined I was really going to be pissed, but I needed answers.

Getting my phone, I marched out the front door and knocked aggressively on the door. Nothing. The wind was blowing up in pre-storm gusts and I pushed my hair out of my eyes. I knocked again to no answer.

Going back through my house I got my gun, then went out the back door. I peered in the windows of the kitchen. With a start I jumped when I realized there was a man staring out at me.

Max. It was Max.

My entire body went cold and I froze, wanting to blink and make sure I wasn't seeing things but afraid to open my eyes again and there be nothing there. Before I could react and actually do anything, the door opened and an arm grabbed me and hauled me inside. The gun went flying out of my hand.

Instinctively, I fought, but strong arms wrapped around me and pinned my arms at my sides. I would have kicked but then there was a voice in my ear, familiar, echoing the past. "Stop, Miranda. Why are you fighting the love of your life?"

Goose bumps rose all over my flesh. I went still again, shock and memories washing over me. "Max?" I whispered, tears suddenly in my eyes. The timber of his voice was more mocking than I remembered, but his scent, his feel, shoved me backwards in time to countless days and nights when I had felt safe and loved. Proud to be with him.

"The one and only." His arms relaxed slightly. "If I let you go are you going to fight me?"

"Of course not. I didn't know it was you. I just saw a man." That wasn't true but for whatever reason I felt like I needed to say it. Distance myself. I tried to turn but his grip tightened again.

His lips burrowed into my hair. "You look good, Mandy. Sexy." He inhaled a deep breath.

It made me shiver. I was confused that he was here after all these years. And he sounded... predatory. "Where have you been?" I whispered, taking in the stark kitchen around me. It was mostly empty except for a table to my right. "Why haven't you contacted me? We had a plan."

"Things changed. I had to think on the fly." He kissed my head. Then he started to slowly turn me again.

And suddenly I was face-to-face with my ex. Who I had never intended to be my ex. Who I was certain was dead. And everyone else was certain had just run off.

"I thought you were dead." Tears sprung to my eyes. I reached out to touch him, tracing a line down his cheek and over his mouth. He looked older, harder. Thinner. He had a scar under his left eye, straight and sharp. Like a razor blade. There were dark smudges under his eyes, like he hadn't slept well in ages. "I was sure you were dead."

His head tilted. "Sometime I wanted to be." His hand covered mine. "So how do I look?"

I was too stunned to be anything but honest. "Like you're being hunted."

He gave a sharp crack of laughter. "You could say that. But you, on the other hand, look like life is treating you well. You look hot as hell."

Lust had appeared in his eyes and I felt the first tremors of alarm, thawing my icy numbness. "Thank you." It should have been a compliment that made me feel good, but I just felt unnerved.

There was no attraction to him. I was staring at him and I felt no love, no desire. I didn't want to hug or kiss him. What I felt was unease, and an overwhelming sense of anger and sadness and confusion over what I had thought ten minutes ago was love lost. "I don't understand," I said, because I didn't. "Where have you been?"

His thumb stroked the back of my hand on his cheek. "Somewhere safe. Somewhere where I could keep you safe."

I had no idea what that even meant. I dropped my hand. Touching him felt strange, foreign. "Everyone told me you were alive but I said if you were you would have contacted me. It's been five years."

His head cocked. "So because you thought I was dead you decided it's okay to fuck my brother?"

It was like being slapped. All the air whooshed out of my lungs. I was first and foremost stunned. But then I was scared. "What are you talking about?" I whispered, which was a stupid thing to say.

If he had been here, watching, listening, then of course he would know. I wondered who the Conrad guy had been. A lookout? But Max the cat had been a message.

I had never been afraid of Max, but now the chill that rushed over me indicated that my body was aware of what Max was capable of, even if my brain couldn't seem to comprehend it.

Max, his hair shorter now than it had been when we dated, shook his head slowly back and forth. "Don't play dumb. It worked for you when we were together but I'm not buying it now. You're thirty years old."

Bewildered, I just stared at him. "What are you talking about? I never played dumb!" A horrible thought occurred to me. Maybe I just was dumb. Because I wasn't following.

Max took a step back. He bent down and picked up my gun, which had fallen in the doorway when he grabbed me. Suddenly I wished it was still in my hand.

"Mandy. Come on. You were the perfect girlfriend because you knew how to play the dumb blonde. The big tits, the tight ass, the friendly smile. You could make the most badass drug dealer feel like he was safe with me. With us. Because you were guileless. It was an amazing act."

Except it hadn't been an act. I had never known what was going on, until the end. When Max had told me he was being framed. When I was spending the night with him and his apartment was broken into and I pulled the trigger on his gun while Max was in the shower, defending myself against the intruder. I hadn't shot at the man, more over him, as a warning, but it had been terrifying.

The tumblers of the combination lock fell into place mentally. I had given Max a cover. So Alejandro had been right. Max was not a good guy. And I was stupid to put my faith in him.

Yet it didn't make any sense. "Did you love me, Max? Or were you glad to leave me behind?" I couldn't prevent the bitterness from seeping into my voice.

Max leaned against the counter. "Don't be like that, sweetheart. You know I loved you. I still love you, even if you're fucking my brother."

I narrowed my eyes, trying to stay calm. I could hear my frantic breathing, more out of anger than fear right now. "Don't throw that in my face. Not one fucking word in five years? Was I never supposed to have a life? Was I supposed to wait forever? You said you would contact me! You had to know that if you didn't for five whole years, I would assume you were dead."

He held his hands out in a conciliatory manner, as if I were being a hysterical female. "Calm down. Yes, you made a logical assumption. No, I didn't figure you would wait forever. But, I didn't think the guy you would choose would be my brother. You can't blame me for being pissed about that."

"I can blame you for a lot of things." My nostrils flared. "And you still haven't given me any explanation. Why are you creeping around in this empty apartment instead of just announcing yourself?"

"I didn't want to scare you."

That was bullshit. There were better ways to handle a reunion. "You have had me totally on edge. I thought I had a crazy stalker watching me."

"Just me and I'm no stalker."

I crossed my arms over my chest. "I don't believe you. This is all insane."

"You don't believe I'm not a stalker?"

"I don't believe you're hiding out over here just to ease me into the idea that you're still alive. I think you have a plan and since you blew me off for your last plan, I think I'm entitled to know what the hell it is."

"Don't ask questions you don't want the answer to."

"Don't pretend to be an obscure philosopher." I stared him down. This was just completely and utterly surreal. Back in the beginning, when I had been desperate for Max to still be alive, I could have never imagined this outcome.

Max burst out laughing. "Come here, give Daddy some love." He reached for me. "I missed you so damn much, Mandy."

I didn't mean to step into his embrace. I did it by rote, the memory of all those times he had opened his arms for me and I was excited to be there, feeling safe and loved. Suddenly I found myself there again, his arms firmly around me, my head against his chest.

I told myself it was only natural. That I was in shock. That this was a goodbye.

In my heart I knew that. Not only was I shocked, I felt suddenly heavy with regret, weighted down by sadness. I had spent five years with my life on hold for a man who thought my whole personality was an act to assist him in his illegal dealings. It was beyond insulting. With one fell swoop he had managed to destroy the love I had felt for a decade, because the man I had loved wasn't real. I had made him up. Ignored the red flags.

So a hug was more for me than him. I wanted comfort from him. I wanted comfort for my grief as I mourned the loss of everything I had ever known to be true. I clung to him, breathing in his scent. He was thinner than he had been. Or maybe it was because I had become used to Alejandro's overabundance of muscles. Max didn't feel scrawny or frail. Just wiry and lean. Like he was not living a life of luxury.

"I'm so mad at you," I whispered. "It was so hard to have everyone telling me you just left me and me saying you wouldn't do that and now I know you did."

Max stroked my back and kissed the top of my head softly. "I didn't have a choice. You can be mad at me all you want but the reality is I just didn't have a choice."

"You should have taken me with you." Though even as I said it I realized he had given me the biggest gift ever in not having done so. I had a life. Without him. A good life. One built on hard work instead of lies and illegal bullshit. I pulled back slightly, realizing my wounded ego and a sense of betrayal were compelling me to say things I didn't really mean.

Going with Max would have been a disaster. And I didn't want to see him again after today. Ever.

He smiled down at me as I pulled back from him. "Just trust me."

That was the last thing I intended to do. I opened my mouth but before I could say what was in my heart—that answers or not, I wanted Max out of my life this time on my terms—he bent down.

Then he kissed me.

WHEN I GOT back to Miranda's place, still puzzling over the new information Mickey had given me, I found the house empty, cooked fish growing cold on the stove. The sauce that was simmering looked like it hadn't been stirred and was burning. That was odd.

"Miranda?" I called out. I didn't hear the shower running. I went down the hallway. The bathroom and the bedroom were both empty. I pulled out my phone and called her. No answer.

Now I was getting worried. I hadn't noticed if her car was on the street or not, so I flipped the blinds in the living room to check. Her car was two houses down on the street, empty. What the hell?

I went back through the house and out the back door. Sometimes she worried when the cat didn't come back right away. Maybe she went searching for him. But the back yard was empty. I glanced around for any sight of the cat but I didn't see his Royal Furriness either.

When I glanced at the apartment next door I realized there

was movement in the kitchen. Creeping toward the house, what I saw was the back of Miranda's head, a man's hand buried in the blond tresses, his other hand on the small of her back. My nostrils flared. What the fuck was going on?

They were kissing.

Miranda was kissing a guy in the abandoned apartment next door.

Fury welled up inside me. No man should have his hands on her. She was mine.

I was moving towards the door, rage pushing me forward, even as I knew I had no exclusive right to her. We hadn't exchanged promises or words of love and hadn't discussed what would happen beyond thirty days. Yet it still felt like a betrayal. Only made worse by what I saw when they split apart, Miranda turning as if she had heard me. Or maybe sensed my presence moving outside the window.

My brother.

It was my brother she was kissing.

And then I knew that I had been played. I didn't understand the game.

All I knew was that act? The sweet innocent naïve woman with a side of sexy? All a fucking lie. She had to have been in this with Max all along. The girl with the gun.

But because I was furious and because I was an idiot and because I hated Max and wanted to punch him in the damn face, I shoved the back door open and sauntered into the kitchen. "Well, this is cozy."

Max gave me a grin. One that I remembered all too well and despised. It was part smirk part pure arrogance. "Hey, little brother, you piece of shit squatter. What can we do for you?"

Miranda's mouth was gaping open and she looked stunned. She was pale and she snapped her jaw closed and swallowed visibly. "Max is alive," she said, her voice trembling.

I frowned. I couldn't read her reaction. Wouldn't she have known that? "Looks that way." I was wearing a suit from work and I tugged on the lapel, testing how tight my jacket was. I wanted a full swing when I slammed my fist into Max's face. "But give me another five minutes and I'll have him dead on the floor."

Max took a step forward, bumping Miranda's shoulder as he shifted, knocking her to the side. The bastard didn't even stop to help her. The guy had always had the worst manners. "And why would you be attempting to kill me, exactly, Alejandro? You're the one fucking my girlfriend."

I wanted to tell him she wasn't his girlfriend but I wasn't sure of that fact. "Because you're a dick," was my response instead. "Because you have been giving Mom and Dad heartache since you were a kid and you deserve to be put in your place."

His arms were over his chest. Max looked older, harder. Skinny. I had no doubt I could take him. He may have crazy on his side, but I had strength. As his eyes raked over me I could tell he knew it too. I wasn't a teenager any more. I had size on him. But he was holding a gun. This was familiar.

"Give me one reason not to put a bullet in your head right now," he said, his arm raising.

But Miranda screamed and stepped right in front of Max, putting herself directly between us.

"Miranda, move!" I yelled, terrified. "Get the hell out of the way." I was furious with her, but that didn't mean I wanted her hurt.

"Listen to Lover Boy," Max said, staring Miranda down, as he shifted slightly so he could see me in the background. His nostrils were flaring with anger and I wasn't sure if it was directed at me or Miranda or both of us.

"I'm not moving unless you promise not to hurt Alejandro," she said.

I had to admit I was touched. Maybe she did care about me. Maybe it hadn't all been an act. "Thanks, Miranda, but I can handle myself," I said. "I don't need you to make deals on my behalf."

"You should be grateful," Max said. "Because if she wasn't here you'd already be dead."

"Why do you want to kill me?" I had to admit, I was curious.

"Because you're having sex with her, you idiot."

Interesting. I eyed him. "But wasn't that the plan? The con? Because there has to be a con. There always is with you. I just don't get the end game."

Miranda gasped and whirled around. Her jaw had dropped. "A con? You think this was all some scheme on my part? You're an asshole." Her voice trembled in fury. "You're both assholes. For five years I thought Max was dead. I told you that. His being here is a total shock to me and now I have you believing that I'm some con artist who seduced you? Screw you."

Either that was feigned outrage or it was the truth. I wasn't sure which. I wanted to believe her, but I wasn't sure it would be wise to at this point. Not with Max holding a weapon. "What's your side of the story, Max? Did Miranda know where you were?"

Her nostrils flared. She was angry with me, clearly. But that was the least of my concerns.

"It's not really any of your business but I'm feeling nostalgic. It's almost good to see you, brother."

As usual, we differed in opinion.

"No, Miranda didn't know where I was," he added. "I needed to protect her. If she knew anything she would have some people pressing her for information."

"But she knew you were alive."

Max shook his head.

"I already told you that," Miranda snapped. "And I'm leaving. I don't want to see either of you right now. Alejandro, you can come and get your clothes tomorrow."

Hey, now. That was taking a giant leap. I thought it was fair that I would have doubts about what the hell was going on. "Let's talk about this."

"I'm done talking." Miranda started toward the door.

But Max wasn't about to let her leave. I realized that immediately and started toward her at the same time he did. He was closer and even though I moved fast, he yanked her back by the arm. She squawked and then cried out when he slammed her back onto the counter.

Fury rose up inside, red and hot. "Get your fucking hands off of her."

"What are you doing?" Miranda asked Max. There were tears in her eyes. I didn't know if they were from pain or the hurt of betrayal that Max was man-handling her. Or that he had lied to her.

It didn't seem like they had a mutual plan worked out.

Though they had been kissing when I had walked in the house.

Max's grip on Miranda tightened as he leaned forward and got in her face. She tried to ease back away from him. I eyed Max's gun, trying to figure out my next move.

Max was not going to have the last word for once.

I was.

I RECOILED FROM the expression on Max's face. It reminded me of when people are high on drugs. His eyes were glassy and wild, a little crazed. Maybe he was on drugs. I didn't know. All I knew was that this man was a total stranger to me.

I had never been afraid of Max, ever. Now I was.

"What are you doing?" I asked, feeling a fluttering of panic, yet at the same time feeling very pissed off. He had a lot of freaking nerve strolling back into my life and throwing me around. "Back off, Max."

"I can't have you leave, Mandy. You need to help me." His breath was hot on my face. "You know I left because there were guys after me, but what you don't know is that I stole half a million bucks from them three years ago after I got to Mexico."

My back was against the countertop and I gripped it tightly, trying to lean as far away from him as possible. I couldn't even see Alejandro any more but I knew that he would be well aware of the gun in Max's hand.

"What does that mean?" I asked in a low voice. I felt I had to placate him, keep him calm. The gun kept brushing against my leg, and I knew it was loaded, which was terrifying. "Is someone after you?"

I knew Alejandro was probably assessing the situation but he wasn't between me and a potential bullet. There wasn't much he could do. I didn't think Max would kill me, but immediately I realized that was a stupid assumption. I hadn't ever imagined that Max was alive still, let alone that he would yank me by the arm and slam me into the kitchen cabinets.

"Yes, they're after me. You can only hide your identity so long, you know?" He reached out and touched the ends of my hair, lifting it and studying the strands. I was almost positive now he was high on something. His movements were strange, his eyes manic. "But you're going to help me." He raised the gun and ran it down my arm. "Do you understand?"

I swallowed, the enormity of the situation really kicking in. I cursed myself for dropping the damn gun. He was bullying me with my own weapon. "You know I'll help you if I can," I murmured.

"I need you to help me steal from your celebrity friends. I want access to their houses, yachts, parties."

"What?" I blurted out before I could stop myself. "Are you insane? I can't do that!" One, I would never betray a trust like that. Two, he would never get away with it. "There are cameras and codes and it's not like there is just money lying around anyone's house."

"I think your mind is straighter than I even remember," he whispered. "You don't get it."

"I don't." I stared into his eyes, this man I had loved. It was like Pet Semetery by Stephen King. Where a loved one dies and you desperately want them back after they're buried, but when they rise they're different. Distorted. Not right.

Max wasn't right.

A shiver rolled up my spine and settled into the roots of my hair.

"Just do what I tell you to do and everything will be fine, Mandy." His fingers buried in my hair and he twisted the strands painfully. My eyes started to water, blurring my vision. He leaned in farther and farther, so that his forehead touched mine and I was forced to blink.

I was terrified as I contemplated action. I could knee him in the balls but I had the feeling that he would either punch me straight in the face or shoot me. I could hear my frantic breathing and smell the sweet sweat of my fear. I decided my best bet was to get him to back away from me. His back was to Alejandro. Even if Alejandro believed I was in collusion with Max, he would still use the opportunity to tackle Max. He was waiting. I could sense it.

So I had to get myself from Max. After I reassured him. "Kiss me, Max," I whispered. "Please. I need you to love me." The words brought bile up into my throat but I knew I sounded sincere in my pleading. I was pleading. For my life.

The corner of his mouth turned up. "I'm going to do more than kiss you." With gun in hand, he roughly grabbed my breast.

It occurred to me I could die right here, right now, maybe even by accident. If the gun went off...

But suddenly Max was sailing back away from me, removed from my space by Alejandro grabbing the back of his shoulders and tossing him against the wall. Alejandro took his wrist and slammed it down on the table, sending the gun to the floor. For a split second I couldn't remember if the safety was on or not, but there was no gunshot ringing out in the room so I felt the air rush out of my lungs in relief and I ran over to grab it. Max was scrambling for control, trying to get off the wall and reach for the gun, but Alejandro was pounding him with his fist.

Blood flew everywhere when Alejandro connected with Max's nose, the crack audible. There were legs distorting my view as they both moved, Max angling for escape, but I managed to grab the gun with both of my sweaty and slippery hands. I scooted backwards on my ass and screamed, "I have the gun, Alejandro!"

It came out louder and more hysterical than I intended and it snapped me out of my fear. I had the gun. I stood up and pointed it at them. "Max," I said, and this time my voice was even, normal volume. "I'm not keeping your secrets anymore."

He couldn't answer me because he was trying desperately to get a punch in on his brother, but mostly he was deflecting blows.

Alejandro's suit jacket ripped at the shoulder.

I pulled my phone out of my pocket and called 911.

Five years. Five freaking years.

Then he showed up and threatened me? Now that I had the gun I was seething with anger. I felt no need to call off Alejandro.

Max could rot in prison for the rest of his natural life. I shivered as the 911 dispatcher asked what my emergency was. "My ex-boyfriend pulled a gun on me," I said.

And just like that, everything I had ever known about the past shattered, shards of broken glass flinging through the air like the spatter from Max's broken nose.

I realized I didn't know anything about anything.

CHAPTER
12

"L et's go home," I said to Miranda hours later. We were at the police station and all the paperwork had been filed and all the questions answered. I was pissed off and tired and us being inside the apartment next door had complicated matters and led to suspicions about our right to be there.

Miranda had explained that she had a permit to carry and that she hadn't seen Max in five years. She had also explained that Max had been involved with drug dealers and that he had disappeared without telling her where he was going, but that she had known what he was doing.

I had sat there in disbelief. Sweet, innocent Miranda wasn't so damn sweet after all. It also made me understand her stubborn and staunch support of the idea that Max was alive. It was because his living was no surprise to her. She had known all about it.

Seeing him touch her, maul her breast with his filthy asshole grip, had made a rage explode inside me that I had never experienced before. I'd been waiting for the moment when Max was distracted enough that I could take him, but I had never expected to hear her whisper, "Kiss me, Max." Or for him to touch her like that.

This had all been such a fucking mistake. I should have never made her mine after she had already been his.

Miranda glanced at me. She looked exhausted. There were dark smudges under her eyes and her mascara was smeared. Her cheeks were pale and she had her arms crossed over her chest, rubbing her elbows. "Can you just take me to my parents', please? I don't want to go back there tonight."

I opened the door to the parking lot for her and hesitated, not sure what to say. But then I decided after all of this I deserved more than her cool politeness. "No. I'll take you to Lola's. We can stop and pick the cat up."

She shot me a glare. "I don't think it's up to you. I can go where I want."

I had her gun and mine, both released back to us in my waistband and I adjusted them. "Miranda. I'm not going to argue about this and I'm not going to roll over and go quietly. We have a few things to talk about."

"I'm exhausted," she snapped as she went through the door, chin up.

"And you might be pregnant," I said baldly. "So you can give me five fucking minutes. You gave Max five years."

Miranda opened her mouth, then promptly shut it again. She got into the car silently and I did the same. I didn't even know where to begin with this conversation.

But then suddenly she spoke as I pulled out of the parking lot. "Go to Peacock Park. I want to see the water."

It seemed like a weird request to me. "You can see the water at Lola's house."

The look she gave me made my balls tighten.

"Just do it."

"Damn," I said, suddenly amused. "I'm not used to you being bossy. I kind of like it."

"None of this is funny."

That was a huge understatement. "No, it's not."

At the park she didn't wait for me but just started walking towards the water. The sailboats docked at the marina were a cluttered white backdrop against the deep blue of the water. I struggled to find the right words. I was the guy who had never wanted a relationship because I had been waiting—for this woman. For Miranda. So I had learned the language of loving women temporarily. For a night. Maybe two. I knew how to charm and coax and cajole and laugh with a woman. I knew how to make her scream in pleasure.

What I didn't know was how to communicate truth. Genuine emotions.

So I didn't know what to say to Miranda to express the depth of what was going on in my damn heart. Hell, I wasn't even sure I could identity all that jumbled mess myself.

She didn't seem to know what to say either. She sat down on the ground by the edge of the dock, crossing her ankles in front of her and leaning back onto the palms of her hands. I sat beside her and raised my knees, resting my arms on them. My suit was wrinkled and I wished I were wearing nothing but my underwear. I wanted to wash the whole damn day off of me.

Miranda sighed. Then she finally spoke. "All I wanted was a baby."

And fuck if that didn't hurt. I didn't want it to hurt, but it did. She hadn't ever wanted me. Not really. Same old shit. Max got trust and loyalty and I was in his shadow. I hoped they threw the book at him.

"You might have one in nine months," I said. "So I guess it's a win for you." It made my gut clench. I pictured her handing me papers to sign over rights to the kid. That wasn't what I wanted. But at the same time I wasn't sure I wanted to be with Miranda. She had lied to me. About everything.

"I don't think so," she said. "I will probably be ovulating next week."

"Well, good luck with that." I turned to look at her. "I'm out. I'm sorry, Miranda."

She didn't seem surprised but she was upset. She chewed her fingernail. "I thought you wanted thirty days."

"I did. But I thought you were being honest with me."

"I was honest with you, Alejandro. I didn't lie to you."

"You just left out the whole fact that you knew all about Max's shady shit and that you were even involved in planning his disappearing act so he wouldn't go to prison. That's a lot different from you pretending for five years to be scared that he was dead."

Miranda pursed her lips. "I wasn't pretending. I really thought he was dead."

I wanted to explode. To demand she admit once and for all Max was a prick but I realized that deep down it didn't matter. What mattered was that her heart was a vault and I had no entry to it. No damn code. She had me shut out and she always had. I had been nothing but an idiot. "Too bad he's not. You could have milked that abandoned widow shit forever."

"That's a shitty thing to say."

I picked up a rock and tossed it into the water, needing motion. I felt restless. Maybe I would go work out after I took her somewhere safe. "What do you want me to say? I walked in on the woman I love and my brother kissing. I'm not in the best of moods."

Though there was a horrible nagging thought in the back of my head that if I didn't know Miranda, could I really love her?

"He caught me off guard. He kissed me, not the other way around. Then I realized I had to placate him, so I just let it happen."

"Like you just let this happen?" I gestured between me and her. She had never said she loved me other than the first night, and she had meant this as a big sister kind of love. She had never even said she wanted to be with me. Not really. "For the record, I'm not criticizing that. But I needed the truth, that's all."

"Well, I needed you to trust that I wouldn't have set you up like some common con artist. I can't believe you would think that of me."

I had nothing to say to that. Not really. I didn't feel bad for my reaction because it was a fair one. Max had always been between us and he still was, unfortunately. I just reached out and touched her knee, running my thumb over it, knowing this was the last time I would ever be able to touch her. We had done this whole thing backwards and now we had nothing. We both knew it.

That was why we had stilted words, a physical distance between us, and gazes that were more comfortable on the water than on each other. "I'm sorry," I told her, and I meant that. I really did. "I pushed you into sex and I'm sorry for that. It was selfish of me."

She shook her head, her cheeks staining pink. "No, I'm sorry for asking you something so monumental like it was no big deal. It's not something to be taken lightly and I never meant to take advantage of your feelings for me."

While the politeness between us made me want to scream, to grab her and push her down and kiss her until she gave me everything, at the same time I was grateful for it because it meant that our need to preserve a friendship of some kind was greater than our anger. I wanted that. We would be those sort-of friends who never saw each other, but I wanted her to understand if she ever needed me, I'd be there in a heartbeat. "If you ever need anything, you can call me. You know that, right?"

She nodded. "Do you want to know if... I mean, there might be papers to sign and..."

I held up my hand. There was a fucking lump in my throat and I didn't want to hear it all spelled out. I didn't want to picture a baby with blond hair on her hip while she cooked in that turquoise kitchen. A happy home that I didn't belong in. "Just send me what you need to. I'll sign it." I didn't want to complicate things for her. I knew she would be an amazing mother. Maybe I had given her that gift. I knew she had given me a gift. A week with her was more than I had ever expected, even if now I knew she had been holding back on me.

"I do love—"

But I cut her off. I knew she was going to say that she loved me. I didn't want that love. Not the friendship, brotherly love. Not even a little bit. I wanted all or I wanted nothing. "You don't have to say anything. Let's just not say anything else."

There was a tear running down her cheek. "I don't understand how we got here."

I wiped it off and leaned in to kiss her forehead softly. I wasn't going to tempt myself with her lips. "It's all good, baby." I stood up and held my hand out to her.

She took it and stood up, wiping her hands on her ass. "I'd rather go to Lola's actually, if you don't mind dropping me off there. I want to be alone and my parents will have a bunch of questions."

"No problem. That makes me feel better because that house has decent security." I went to brush her hair back then stopped myself. "I still don't know what is up with that apartment next door. Max didn't explain what the hell is actually going on."

"Everything that I thought was wrong," she whispered. "That's why I'm afraid. I don't know what to believe."

I wasn't sure what she meant and I didn't want to dig further and find out. I just nodded. Then I started toward the car, opening the passenger door for her. I turned on music and let the sound swell up and around us, preventing any further conversation. I knew she was crying. I could sense it without looking at her. Her shoulders were shaking and I wanted to comfort her, but at the same time I had no comfort to give if she was crying over Max.

It wasn't in me. I wanted her to cry over me. Over losing me. But she wouldn't. And that shit hurt. So I stared at the road, and drove too fast, and barely glanced at her when I walked her to the door at Lola Brandy's house. The house where we had spent the night wrapped in each other's arms on the couch.

"Alejandro," she said, drawing my name out with naked longing. There was sadness and pleading in that tone and I suddenly despised my name. On everyone else's lips it was a party name. On hers it sounded sweet and sensual.

It pissed me off. "You picked the wrong Garcia brother," I told her after she stepped inside.

Then when she would have responded, I reached out and pulled the door shut. I heard the lock click in place and then I got the fuck out of there.

I called Ryan. "Hey, you want to get drunk with me? My

brother just rose from the dead, man."

I KNEW ALEJANDRO was angry with me and hurt but I couldn't give him what he needed. Not when my own emotions were a horrible mix of betrayal and anger and fear and disgust. He wasn't being sympathetic enough to the fact that everything I had thought about my relationship with Max was just gone. *Poof.* I felt like the world's biggest naïve idiot.

So when Alejandro pulled the door shut in my face I didn't bother to go after him. I couldn't make him feel better right now. I couldn't even make me feel better. Cheeks stained with tears, I wandered into Lola's living room and stared out the windows at the pool. The water shimmered under the lights. I popped the slider open and stood there with my arms around my chest.

I didn't know what to do or how to process everything that I had learned. After a minute I called Zoe, who I hadn't spoken to since brunch at her parents', despite her repeatedly texting me.

"Hey," she said. "I'm glad you called."

Her voice sounded concerned. "Are you busy?"

"No. How are you? Is everything okay?"

"I need to apologize to you. Can you come over?"

"Of course. And you don't need to apologize. I shouldn't have blurted it out like that. What the hell does it even matter anymore?"

"Oh, it matters. I'm at Lola Brandy's house in North Beach.

How soon can you be here?"

"I get to hang at a pop star's house? Shut the fuck up."

That made me laugh. "Yes."

I gave her the address and while I was waiting for her I went to sit by the pool, slipping off my sandals so I could dip my toes in. I could see Alejandro everywhere here, smiling at me. But then Max's face would appear in my thoughts, his eyes crazy and intense. I shivered.

Impulsively I went and deleted my screen saver shot of him. Then I scrolled through the pictures I had of him. I had always thought he was smiling at the camera, or in one particular picture, staring adoringly at me. Now as I studied it, I interpreted it differently.

My hair was straighter and flatter than the style of the time and I had on a neon pink crop top. Which in hindsight wasn't a fabulous fashion choice but I had been maybe twenty-three in the picture. I could get away with it. We'd been at a bar in the Grove because Max didn't go to clubs. He hated South Beach. That was more Alejandro's scene. Max didn't like people. But he would go to a bar with me if it had dark corners and sticky floors.

In this photo I was staring out at the camera, smiling broadly, so happy he had agreed to accompany me for a night out. Max wasn't looking at the camera at all. He was looking at me. I had always thought it was a romantic moment captured. He had been gazing down at me, the woman he loved beyond measure.

Funny how having him wave a gun in my face could change that.

Now it looked predatory.

I suddenly felt anger bubble up inside me and burst forth. I hurled my cell phone across the patio, feeling a sick satisfaction when it made contact with the concrete wall of the house. It dropped to the tile floor.

When I went and retrieved it, my phone was fine, but the screen was shattered. Max's face was splintered. My smile was sliced in half.

That seemed about right.

"Max is alive," I told Zoe, after we sat down by the pool in chaise lounge chairs. I had given her a quick tour and she had gushed over the house and how cool it was to be there, but then she had told me to tell her what was up.

There was no sense beating around the bush.

Her eyes widened. "What? How do you know?"

"Because tonight he was in the apartment next door to me and he pulled a gun on me."

"Oh shit."

Basically. "He's been watching me. He wants me to help him steal from my celebrity contacts. When I said no, the gun went in my face." I shivered, just not quite able to wrap my head around what had happened.

Zoe had brought a bottle of tequila and she held it out to me. "Jesus. Take a swig."

I shook my head. "I can't. I might be pregnant."

Her eyes widened. "What the hell happened in the last nine

days? You don't waste time, girl."

"I had sex with Alejandro." My cheeks burned at the memory. "Actually, I had a lot of sex with Alejandro. Like maybe fifteen times." I thought about it. "Or twenty." I put my hands on my cheeks to cool my skin.

"That's a lot of sperm." She sipped the tequila. "I'm sorry, I need to wrap my head around all of this. So like what, you guys are dating?"

I shook my head. "He thinks that I had some evil plot going with Max this whole time so he was pissed at me, then I got pissed at him for thinking I could be a jerk like that."

"But that aside, how do you feel about him?" She eyed me, cradling her booze bottle against her chest. "I mean, he's potentially the father of your child. Was it all just baby-making sex, or was there something more?"

I took a deep breath, prepared to give the answer on the tip of my tongue—that of course there was something more, that I cared about Alejandro, and respected him. But then I pictured him watching me, with deep admiration and love, and I knew it was more than that. He was a good man, who made me laugh and who always had my back. Who would stick. If I let him. Love swelled up inside me, deep and unhurried and mature. "I love him," I whispered, tears appearing out of nowhere. "I really do. Is that bad?"

Zoe laughed. "I mean, it's only bad if you don't want to love him."

Swallowing, I wiped my eyes. "No. I do want to love him. But I want to start over and do this right. Without the shadow of Max hanging over us or me wanting to have a baby."

My best friend reached out and squeezed my hand. "Hey. There are no do-overs. Own your shit. Take a minute. Figure out what you really want. Then make it happen. You're no dumb blonde. You know what you're doing."

"Thanks for the confidence but I'm pretty sure I've never known what I was doing. I was totally fooled by Max."

"What did he look like, by the way?"

"High as a kite and like life has kicked him in the dick a few times." It was true.

"Good," Zoe said with relish. "Though I wouldn't mind kicking him in the dick for real for what he's done to you. And where the fuck was he?"

"Mexico." Did I want to kick Max in the dick? I thought about it. Anger wasn't usually my style. I tended to forgive far too easily. But I didn't want to forgive Max. I wanted him to give me back my innocence and the last five years of my life.

But Zoe was right. There were no do-overs. I could let this break me or I could get the hell over it and finally move on the way everyone had been urging me to for years.

"I can't believe my ass is sitting on Lola Brandy's lounge chair. This is so awesome. Just as a side note." She wiggled around on the chair like she wanted to absorb the mojo.

It made me laugh. I stood up. "You know what I need to do? I

need to jump in this pool and wash Max off of me once and for all."
I stripped down to my bra and panties. It felt liberating.

I had skinny dipped here with Alejandro but this was different.
This was shedding layers of the past, not my inhibitions. This was a
soul cleanse. This was me forgiving myself for loving Max.

Diving in I let the cool water embrace me.

I knew I had to tell Alejandro everything, even if it embarrassed
me. Even if it meant he would never speak to me again.

THE NEXT DAY, hungover as fuck, I went down to the police station
and posted bail for Max just so I could punch him again. He
refused to get in the car with me.

"Fuck you, I'm walking," he said, when I yelled at him to get
in the car.

"Pussy."

"Suck my dick." He was heading north out of the parking lot.

"You let me bail you out but you won't get in my car?" I had a
throbbing headache and a bad attitude. "Fine. Walk, though I can't
imagine where you're going unless it's to hell."

He stopped walking and glared back at me, his face bruised
from our fight the day before. "Stop pretending like you've been so
goddamn injured. I never did shit to you, Alejandro."

I rubbed the top of my head, hoping to ease the pain in
my skull. I had torn it up at the clubs the night before, and had

consumed more vodka than was advisable. "You're a piece of work, you know that? My whole childhood was about you. Mom and Dad were always walking on eggshells hoping you didn't explode. It was all about you."

He scoffed. "Grow up. You're not eight anymore."

I started toward him but he darted to the right. "Dude, go ahead. We're in the police station parking lot. You'll have assault charges on you right next to me."

He was right and I wasn't about to give him that satisfaction. "You're not worth it. I'm done with you. You may not be dead but you're dead to me. I bailed your sorry ass out and if you have any sense of decency at all you'll leave Mom and Dad and Miranda alone from here on out." I was worried about my parents. They were going to be heartbroken when they found out he just hadn't contacted them in five years. But I had to tell them. No more secrets in our family. No more lies.

"That's ridiculously dramatic." Max held his hand out. "Give me a hundred bucks and I'll leave Miranda alone."

I froze. He hit a nerve and he knew it. He goaded me. "You like her, don't you? You like your brother's cast offs?"

My fist shot out and nailed him straight in the gut, because I wanted to see him double over. He groaned.

"Is that all you got?" he asked, drawing himself back up. He looked beat to hell, tired, older than his thirty years.

"No, but you know what? I'm going to leave it at that. You're my brother, even if that means nothing to you. It does still mean something to me." I could say that Max was dead to me, but it didn't change anything. We were connected and always would be. We shared a mutual history and I couldn't erase the past.

Max cocked his head. He looked like he didn't know what to make of my words. "And what does it mean? That you're going to invite me over to dinner? You, me, and Miranda? No, thanks."

Something about his tone made me curious. "Does it really bother you that she and I started something? I wouldn't think you would care, honestly." I didn't. "For the record, it had nothing to do with you. I wasn't trying to get back at you by seeing Miranda. I've always wanted to be with her, it's that simple. But I didn't think you would care one way or the other."

"Of course I care," he snapped. "Look, I may not be perfect but I do have fucking feelings."

I wasn't sure I believed him. "That's reassuring," I said dryly. But I reached into my wallet and I gave him twenty bucks. "Get yourself a ride. Do what you need to do."

Max shook his head. "I don't need your money." He stuck his hand out. "See you around, man. Take care of Miranda."

I was suspicious of him and his words, but I decided it didn't matter. "Miranda isn't mine to take care of. She's her own woman." I took his hand and firmly shook it. "Be safe."

"You too, bro." He gave me an enigmatic smile. "I'm either going to disappear again or I'll end up in prison. Either way, I'll probably never see you again."

I just nodded and he walked away. It was more closure than I had ever expected to have. Despite how angry I was with him for threatening Miranda, I was ready to be done with the past.

Getting in my car and driving away, I called Miranda. I wasn't sure if she would pick up or not but I needed to talk to her about a restraining order against Max, just to be safe.

"Hello?" Her voice was soft, tentative.

"Hey. I'm sorry to bother you, but I wanted to let you know Max is out on bail. I think you should file a restraining order against him."

She paused. "I don't know if that's such a good idea. I don't want to piss him off."

"I think he's already pissed off." I headed toward home. I needed a shower to wash away the stink of my late night. Drinking that much had been stupid but I had been too torn up over Miranda to be rational. I hadn't even enjoyed myself. Women had flirted with me and whereas in the past I would have loved every minute of that, I hadn't been able to get the image of Miranda naked, shattering below me, out of my head. I couldn't have sex with another woman. Not yet.

"The thing is that if I turn on him, he'll turn on me. I was there, Alejandro. I found out that Max was dealing drugs, and I didn't do anything about it." There was a pause and she added, "I transported for him twice. It was so stupid, I know, but I didn't know what else to do. He would have been so mad at me if I didn't and I was so young and naïve. But if I file a restraining order, he might tell the cops about that."

I believed she was telling the truth. Miranda was a trusting person. "Did you ever think that you were in an emotionally abusive relationship? I'm being serious. Max had you completely under his control." It made me wish again for the thousandth time I had done something about it. I should have stolen her from Max back in the day. But that thought made me roll my eyes. Because a twenty-year-old woman was going to dump her boyfriend for his fifteen-year-old brother.

"Maybe. I never thought about it in those terms. But I am still responsible for my actions. I feel guilty that I wasn't stronger. I was going to meet up with him, you know. We made a plan. I was going to run with him like some Bonnie and Clyde fantasy."

"I'm glad you didn't."

"Me, too. And you're right. I need to file a restraining order. There is nothing that he can do to me that I can't handle. Besides, if he has dirt on me, I have more on him."

"That's my girl." I was proud of her for finally standing up to him. She had allowed him to dominate her life far too long. "Let me know if you want me to go to the station with you."

"I'll be fine, but thank you." Her voice was soft. "Thank you for everything."

I had a lump in my throat and it wasn't from the drinking. "Yeah. Talk to you later."

We hung up and that was that.

That night I went out drinking again and I made out with a brunette who looked nothing like Miranda.

CHAPTER
13

"Don't throw up," I coached myself as I parked in Alejandro's driveway and smoothed the front of my sundress down. My palms were damp and my heart was racing. I lifted the bakery box off the passenger seat and exited my car.

I didn't think I would actually puke, but after three months of morning sickness I had come to expect the urge to hit at random intervals for various reasons. Zoe had been right—it had been a lot of sperm. Even though I had thought it was a little early for ovulation I had wound up pregnant.

For three months I had kept my mouth shut because I had been terrified to miscarry after telling Alejandro, especially since I wasn't sure what his reaction would be. So I decided to wait for the second trimester to share the news with him.

Amazed, I had been navigating the nausea and the idea that I was going to be a mother with some hard-core soul searching and healing. Alejandro's words about Max being emotionally abusive had caused me to really dig into his emotions and my behaviors. I needed to have my head on straight before this baby was born.

I also knew that I loved Alejandro. He was a good man, who cared about people in general, and I admired and respected him.

So here I was, surprising him with a cake on his birthday, planning to make a plea that we should give it a go. My stomach flipped again. Maybe this was the world's stupidest idea. I contemplated leaving the cake on his doorstep and bolting but that was a cop out.

His front door opened and he appeared, shirtless and sweaty. "Miranda?"

Too late to run. And I had a sudden horrible thought that he was bare-chested and out of breath because he was in the middle of having sex with a woman. A birthday bang. I cleared my throat. That would be awkward as hell and make me hideously jealous, but it was possible. Alejandro was a favorite of the club girls. I knew that.

I had to brazen it out. "Hi," I said, walking toward him in my heels. I had chosen a white sundress with red cherries on it and stable wedge heel sandals. The dress gave me good cleavage, and I could already see his eyes drifting to my breasts. "Am I interrupting you?"

Holding my breath, I waited for his response. To my relief, he shook his head, lifting his gaze to meet mine. "No, I was just working out. Come on in." He stepped back to let me into his apartment.

Alejandro looked sexy as hell. Hard as a rock and I remembered what he was capable of doing with all those muscles. How he had held me against the wall and driven me crazy. I felt the fluttering of desire. I stared at his ass as he walked down the hall. I had been a lucky woman to experience that body up against mine and I wanted it again.

He gestured to his couch. "Have a seat." His voice was polite. I could tell he was curious but waiting for me to explain. He held his hands out. "Can I take that from you?"

"Happy Birthday!" I said in a cheerful singsong voice. "I baked you a cake."

"Really?" He smiled. "Thank you. That was really sweet of you. God, I can't believe you remembered."

"It's *Dulce de Leche*. I remember you said that's your favorite."

"Yes." He looked downright excited. He set it down on the coffee table. "Can I have some now? Do you want a piece?"

"Sure." I was going to die if he didn't actually open that box. I was waiting impatiently for him to see my message.

Fortunately he did open the box instead of going for plates and a knife first. "Happy Birthday, Daddy," he said. "Uh, babe, I think you gave me the wrong cake. Unless that's supposed to be you hitting on me."

I just waited. I knew he would figure it out and he did a split second later. His head snapped up. "Wait, does this mean you're pregnant? Are we having a baby?"

His eyes were huge. I nodded, tears of happiness springing to my eyes. "Yes. Twelve weeks. I wanted to wait until the second trimester to tell you just to make sure everything was going to be okay. So thank you, Alejandro, from the bottom of my heart."

"You're welcome. Damn, I can't believe it. You thought it was the wrong time."

"I was wrong about it being wrong." I reached out and touched his arm. "And I want you to be involved if you want to." I searched his face, wanting some kind of a sign of encouragement. But mostly he looked stunned. "I want you to be involved with the baby and me, if that's what you want."

I had rehearsed this speech a million times and in my head it had sounded much better. Now it seemed weird and desperate. But it was out, just hanging there.

His eyebrows shot up. "Why?" he asked. "Why me?"

It was what he had asked me three months ago when I had made my request for a baby. I gave him the same answer. "Because I love you." I leaned forward, raising my hand to his cheek. "I really truly love you. I think you're an amazing, caring man, and I would like us to be together. Forever. With our baby. If you want to. But I don't know if you want this, if I can have this, you and me." Damn it. I was babbling now.

His hand covered mine and for a split second I was worried he would remove it. But instead he turned and kissed my fingers. "Baby, you had me when I was fifteen years old. You've always had me. People always want to know why I don't have serious relationships and it's always been because I was waiting for you. You've always been my ultimate."

My heart soared. "Really?"

He nodded. "Really." He pulled my face to his and gave me a soft kiss. "I love you."

I just about jumped into his lap. I was absolutely sure I had never been so happy in my entire life. "You do?" He had told me before, but that he would tell me now, after everything, made me feel amazing. This was it. We were doing this.

"I do." He pulled me down onto his thighs and cupped my cheeks. "You are so beautiful." His hands drifted down to my still flat belly. "I can't believe there is a baby in there. My baby. Our baby."

"Are you happy?" That definitely worried me. I wanted him to want this as much as I did. "You're kind of young to have a baby," I teased him.

That made him laugh. "Not too young to make a baby, obviously. And clearly, I have some serious mojo in the baby-making department. So yeah, you're welcome."

He was having a proud man moment, his chest a little puffed up. After everything, I could certainly let him have that. "Very impressive, I have to say. I thought it would take months and months."

"Well now we can have worry-free sex for the next six months." He touched the swell of my breast. "And I think we should start now because I feel like you wore this dress to tempt me, and it's working."

"Don't you want a piece of cake first?" I asked, already getting turned on by his finger tracing back and forth over my tender flesh.

"No. I want a piece of you first." He bent over and sucked my breast. "Your tits are huge, baby. They were amazing before but now they are seriously like a magnet. I can't stop looking and touching."

"I have a lot of things you can touch," I murmured, my head falling back in ecstasy as he pulled my nipple into his mouth.

We were impatient and eager for each other and we grappled at clothes desperately. Fortunately he wasn't wearing a shirt and I had a dress on, so within a minute I was resting on his cock, full of him in all ways possible.

I HAD THOUGHT my birthday was going to be pretty ordinary. My only plans were poker with the guys later and maybe a six-pack. But I had glanced out my window and seen Miranda standing there looking like a pinup girl, and now ten minutes later she was riding my cock with some serious enthusiasm and we were together. Having a baby.

Happy Fucking Birthday to me. Literally.

"I like your cherries," I told her, gripping her waist to help her lift up and down on my hard cock. I flicked my tongue over both her nipple and a cherry on the fabric below it. "Very juicy."

She gave a breathless laugh. "You make me feel very juicy."

"You are very, very wet." Her body was an absolute thing of beauty. It should have felt surreal but it didn't. In fact, it felt like this was the way it was always supposed to be. Like the last three months I had known we would get here when we needed to.

"And you're so huge." Her cheeks were pink. "Honey, this feels different, like I have more sensation or something. Oh damn, I'm going to come already."

That made me groan. "Do it, baby. Come for me."

She did, with her head thrown back and her breasts bouncing. She was gorgeous and I knew I was the luckiest son of a bitch alive. It didn't take me long after that either. It had been three long months celibate, probably the longest stretch in my whole life, but I hadn't wanted to be with anyone but Miranda. I exploded inside her.

After she stopped moving, I was overwhelmed by the intensity of what I felt for her. My woman. "Hey," I said. "You still owe me the rest of my thirty days."

Miranda laughed. "I think that can be arranged. I have finally unpacked so things are more comfortable at my place."

She had told me that the guy next door was gone. He had been with vice, watching her, because he knew Max was back in town. My brother had a whole laundry list of crimes they were trying to bust him for, including armed robbery in Texas, and a homicide. He was going to spend the rest of his life in prison. Miranda said a young couple had moved in to the empty apartment and they were nice, which reassured me.

"So maybe we can finish out my thirty days and you can decide if you want to keep me around or not." I brushed my thumb over her bottom lip.

She shook her head. "Nah. I already know. I want you with me always."

"Then I think you should marry me." I wasn't dicking around. I wanted this locked in. Ten years was long enough to wait.

"I think I should," she said, with the world's cutest, most seductive smile. "Though I will not be telling our child you proposed to me while still buried inside me."

I grinned. "Good point. Well, let me cut my birthday cake and I'll do it better."

But she just sighed and wiggled on my cock. "Hmm. In a minute. This feels so good."

"Remember when you said you didn't miss the heat in Miami?" I gave her ass a light spank. "You were lying." I was growing hard again and she knew it.

Her eyes darkened. "You're right, because I do like your heat."

"This is the best birthday ever."

But she just shook her head and smiled at me. "They're only going to get better from here on out because we'll be together. You, me, and baby Garcia."

I couldn't think of anything better.

I like women. But I only love one.

OTHER SERIES BY
ERIN McCARTHY

South Beach Bodyguards Series
BURN

BREAK

HEAT

BLURRED LINES SERIES
Download the first book in this series, You Make Me, for FREE!!
You Make Me

Live For Me

Let Me In

Meant for Me

Breathe Me In

The True Believers Series
True

Sweet

Believe

Shatter

ABOUT THE AUTHOR

USA Today and New York Times Bestselling author Erin McCarthy sold her first book in 2002 and has since written almost seventy novels and novellas in teen fiction, new adult, and adult romance. Erin has a special weakness for tattoos, high-heeled boots, Miami Beach, Frank Sinatra, and martinis. She lives with her husband and their blended family of kids and rescue dogs.

You can find Erin on Facebook, Twitter, or on Goodreads. Or visit her website at www.erinmccarthy.net.